"Wow. You *are* a strong one," Roxie said to Fig.

He smiled a genuinely pleased smile and winked. "Remember that." He moved closer on his way to discard his gloves in the trash can and whispered, "Dream about it."

"As if any part of you registers with my subconscious." Especially not his head—in the dream where she was a cat sleeping curled around it. Or his laugh, or the teasing twinkle in his green eyes, or the contagious smile that brightened his handsome face.

Something about him made her feel safe, as if she could let her guard down. Thank goodness she hadn't. He also made her want…things she didn't usually crave without a couple of beers on board. Was it his slow, laid-back demeanor and quiet confidence? His quick, dry sense of humor? His build—a perfect complement to her large frame? His distinctive look or his air of reserved power?

Whatever it was it gave her an unsettling schoolgirl crush sort of feeling. And Roxie didn't like it.

Dear Reader

This is the third and final (at least for now) book in my *Madrin Memorial Hospital* series: Roxie's story. If you're unfamiliar with the first two books, please check out Book One, Allison's story, WHEN ONE NIGHT ISN'T ENOUGH, and Book Two, Victoria's story, ONCE A GOOD GIRL…

For me, a story builds from a few random ideas—usually jotted down on napkins, receipts, and/or scraps of paper that clutter my pocketbook and desk. After I come up with a few key scenes, and figure out the basics of what I want to happen in the beginning, middle and end, I start to flesh out my characters.

This is my favourite part of the writing process. Beyond their physical characteristics I delve into their pasts. I create their personalities and mannerisms, their goals and motivations. And the more time I spend with them, the more real they become—to the point where they often take on a life of their own, sending my story in a direction different from the one I'd originally intended.

All three women in this series had difficult childhoods, and had to overcome many obstacles on their way to becoming strong, self-sufficient, professional young nurses. I'm happy to have helped each of them find their happily-ever-after.

As I put the final touches on Roxie's story I realised how much I'm going to miss spending my days (and nights) with my friends at Madrin Memorial Hospital. I hope you've enjoyed reading Allison, Victoria and Roxie's stories as much as I've enjoyed writing them.

I love to hear from readers. Please visit me at www.WendySMarcus.com

Wishing you all good things

Wendy S. Marcus

THE NURSE'S NOT-SO-SECRET SCANDAL

BY
WENDY S. MARCUS

First published in Great Britain 2012
by Mills & Boon, an imprint of Harlequin (UK) Limited.
Large Print edition 2012
Harlequin (UK) Limited, Eton House,
18-24 Paradise Road, Richmond, Surrey TW9 1SR

© Wendy S. Marcus 2012

ISBN: 978 0 263 22477 1

Harlequin (UK) policy is to use papers that are natural, renewable and recyclable products and made from wood grown in sustainable forests. The logging and manufacturing process conform to the legal environmental regulations of the country of origin.

Printed and bound in Great Britain
by CPI Antony Rowe, Chippenham, Wiltshire

Wendy S. Marcus is not a lifelong reader. As a child, she never burrowed under her covers with a flashlight and a good book. In senior English she skimmed the classics, reading the bare minimum required to pass the class. Wendy found her love of reading later in life, in a box of old paperbacks at a school fundraiser where she was introduced to the romance genre in the form of a Harlequin Superromance. Since that first book she's been a voracious reader of romance, oftentimes staying up way too late to reach the happy ending before letting herself go to sleep.

Wendy lives in the beautiful Hudson Valley region of New York, with her husband, two of their three children, and their beloved dog Buddy. A nurse by trade, Wendy has a master's degree in Healthcare Administration. After years of working in the medical profession she's taken a radical turn to write hot contemporary romances, with strong heroes, feisty heroines, and lots of laughs. Wendy loves hearing from readers. Please visit her blog at www.WendySMarcus.com

Recent titles by the same author:

ONCE A GOOD GIRL…
WHEN ONE NIGHT ISN'T ENOUGH

**These books are also available in eBook format
from www.millsandboon.co.uk**

Dedication

This book is dedicated to my dear neighbors,
Grisel DeLoe and D. David Dick, two of my biggest
supporters, and a heck of a lot of fun to celebrate with.
(Although after my 4 star *RT Book Reviews* celebration
I had some trouble getting started the next day!)
I love you both. And if you try to sell your house I
may have to resort to vandalism. You have been warned!

With special thanks to:

Grisel and her sister, Ivette Vazquez,
who answered my last-minute cries for help
with some Spanish translations. Your e-mails made me
laugh out loud. Even at three in the morning. You are
one hysterical woman. Any mistakes are my own.

My editor, Flo Nicoll, who encourages me,
puts up with me, and always pushes me to do my best.
I am so lucky to have you.

My wonderful friends, old and new,
who have purchased my books, written reviews, and/or
attended my book signings. You know who you are.

And to my husband and children for loving me, cooking
for me and making me laugh. (And for not saying one
negative word when I spent a weekend in my pajamas
and didn't shower for almost three whole days
while under deadline to finish this book.)

CHAPTER ONE

"It's not Roxie," 5E head nurse Victoria Forley insisted. The tiny brunette slammed the file in her hand onto her old metal desk. "She's one of my best nurses, and a dear friend. I trust her implicitly. This is absolutely ridiculous."

"Calm down, honey," her fiancé, Dr. Kyle Karlinsky, said as he wrapped his large arm around her narrow shoulders. "We'll figure it out."

Ryan "Fig" Figelstein leaned against the door frame of Victoria's fifth-floor office, watching the cozy scene. An observer. An outsider in his best friend's new life.

Kyle shot over the look that more often than not got Fig into some kind of trouble and added, "And Fig will help us."

"Ooohhh, no." Fig held up both hands. "Come see where I work, you said, just for a few minutes." Kyle knew how much Fig hated hospitals.

The smells. The sounds. The isolation and depri-vation. He staved off a shudder.

"You okay?" Kyle asked, studying him, able to read Fig better than anyone.

"Yeah." Fig pushed off the door frame and took a step into the tiny office. "So what's your idea?" he asked to get the focus off of him.

"You're here another week, right?" Kyle asked.

"That's the plan."

"It's perfect." Kyle rubbed his hands together.

Perfect would be them leaving the hospital. Now. Perfect would be an end to his mother's constant telephone calls and ploys for his attention. Perfect would be some sense of normalcy in a life that was feeling increasingly out of his control.

"You hire on here. As the unit clerk."

"Are you…?"

Before he could get out the word *crazy* Kyle added, "Just hear me out." His voice took on that placating tone he used every time he set out to convince Fig to do something he didn't want to do. Kyle removed his arm from Victoria and set his full attention on Fig. "You answer the phone, respond to the call bells, direct visitors."

"It takes more than that…" Victoria started.

"And he watches Roxie and the narcotic cabinet," Kyle added to silence her. "Each time she or someone else accesses it he'll call you."

"You're brilliant," Victoria said to Kyle with a big grin. Then she turned to Fig. "You have to take the job," she pleaded. "Each day I have a different temp circulating through. I need a person I can trust to keep an eye on Roxie. Something's going on. She's been forgetful and distracted. She doesn't have her normal spunk."

Signs of drug abuse. Fig glanced at Kyle.

Victoria caught him. "She's not on drugs. Please," she said, looking up at Fig in that way women do when they have no intention of accepting no for an answer.

"I work with computers." And he was damn good at it. In demand even. "I have a job."

"But you can work anywhere," Kyle pointed out, oh, so helpfully.

"I'm not a big fan of sick people," he admitted. Some deep-seated fears were not easy to get past. "And I know nothing about being a unit clerk in a hospital." Frankly, the thought of spending twelve captive hours in one left him cold and clammy.

"You're not expected to have any physical contact with the patients. And I'll train you myself," Victoria said. "I'll help out as much as I can and I'll tell my nurses to pitch in, too. The narcotic cabinet is in a locked room right behind the desk where you'll be sitting. All you need to do is report any suspicious behavior and I'll check the Demerol count."

"I've got an idea," Fig said. "If you're so certain Roxie had nothing to do with the missing drugs, why don't you tell her what's up and ask her if she knows anything?" Fig preferred the straightforward approach, hated when people danced around an issue.

"Normally I would, and as her friend I want to." Victoria looked torn. "But my job requires I remain objective and investigate the matter fully. Which is what I'm trying to do. Please say you'll help me."

"We can spend more time together." Kyle smiled. "And you'll be earning nine dollars an hour to boot."

Like Fig needed the money. "Seriously," Kyle said. "This means a lot to Victoria so it means a lot to me. You're here. You're impartial. You have no vested interest in Roxie's guilt or innocence."

Now, that wasn't entirely true. In the few hours he'd spent with her at last week's Employee of the Month dinner to honor Kyle, Fig found Roxie to be a total hoot. He liked her. Really liked her. And would rather not participate in any activity that may turn out to be detrimental to her well-being. Not to mention after pulling a no-show for their date Friday night, Fig was not looking forward to Roxie setting eyes on his alive self. The woman had a sharp wit and, per her own admission, an even sharper temper.

But then Kyle added, "I trust you, my closest friend, to help prove Roxie's innocence."

And Fig was sunk. Over the past eight years— since rooming with Kyle at the physical rehab after his "accident"—Kyle had been like a brother, building Fig's confidence and helping him through the most difficult time in his life. How could he say no to the man who'd improved his quality of life to the point it felt worth living?

"I know I'm going to regret this," Fig conceded.

"So you'll do it?" Victoria asked, cautiously optimistic.

"Yeah."

"I'll call Human Resources." She picked up the phone. "You can start tomorrow."

Terrific. For the next week Fig was stuck in the Podunk town of Madrin Falls in upstate New York—where he couldn't even get a decent cup of coffee—filling in for the unit clerk on a busy medical-surgical floor at Madrin Memorial Hospital. What did he know about being a clerk? Nothing. But he'd seen enough of them in action to have a pretty good idea of what he'd need to do. And honestly, he was a college-educated professional. How hard could it be?

The next morning at the God-awful hour of way the hell too early, Fig set his two cups of cafeteria "coffee" on the table in the 5E nursing lounge and caught a glimpse of his reflection in the huge window. Obviously the hospital didn't have many six-foot-four-inch unit clerks on staff, because the drab tan uniform jacket they expected him to wear fit like a bolero jacket with three-quarter sleeves.

He peeled it off and tossed it onto a chair. He jogged in place to work off some of his jitters. "You are not a patient," he started his pep talk. "At the end of the day you get to go home." He jumped three times and stretched out each shoulder. "You can do this."

"Well, lookey here. All alone and talking to yourself. Psych ward's on the fourth floor."

He recognized the voice instantly. Roxie Morano. He turned to face her, so as not to leave his back open to attack. Purely precautionary.

"Jeez, woman." He held his arm up to shield his eyes. "You're an assault to early-morning vision." While she wore the lavender scrubs that identified her as 5E nursing staff, she'd chosen a long-sleeve white turtleneck covered in small multicolored stars to go underneath her top. About a dozen colorful cartoon character pins adorned her left breast pocket—which covered an appealing, rounded breast. Red rectangular-framed glasses hung from a purple chain around her neck that tangled with the lime-green cord from which her chunky yellow pen hung. A bright red scrub jacket with bold pink, yellow and blue hearts lay draped over her arm. Farther down she had on red clogs that clashed with a few inches of exposed orange, green and yellow striped socks. Up on her head her kinky cream soda curls were pulled back in a thick, bright orange hair band.

Beyond the distraction of color, Fig took a moment to absorb the beauty of her smooth, tan skin, her warm brown eyes—that looked heavy with exhaustion rather than light with laughter like they'd been on the night they'd met—and the lusciousness of her perfect-for-him body.

"If it isn't Ryan—my friends call me Fig—Figelstein." She walked toward him. "I thought the deal was if you survived the week we'd head out to dinner to celebrate, *Ryan*."

Okay. He got the emphasis she placed on *Ryan*. Point received. He'd have to work to earn back her favor. An effort well worth the anticipated payoff. Her. Naked. In his bed. Which, based on the heated attraction zipping and zapping between them last week, was where they'd been headed. If only someone else had been available to babysit Victoria's son after the dinner. If only he hadn't missed their date.

"When you didn't come," she continued, "I said a prayer, just like I'd promised. I even contemplated attending church on Sunday, and what a ruckus that would have caused." She stalked toward him. "And here you are." She looked him up and down. "Fit as a fiddle."

Her cell phone rang. She looked at the number, let out a frustrated breath and turned away. "What?" she snapped into the device. "I told you no. My answer won't change." She listened. "Fine. Do what you have to do." She slipped the phone back into her breast pocket and turned to him. "So, *Ryan*. I can't begin to imagine what's transpired to make a self-proclaimed computer genius, such as yourself, stoop to the role of hospital clerical worker."

"Anything to get close to you," he said. "So I could apologize for missing our date. Please, we're friends. Call me Fig." Only his mother called him Ryan, because she flat out refused to call him anything else. Ryan represented his old self. The child homeschooled because of his medical conditions, brainwashed to fear the world around him, the tentative, lonely teenager who lacked confidence and had no real friends. Fig—the nickname chosen by Kyle—fit his new and improved self. A man of character who chose to embrace life rather than hide from it, to experience life rather than watch others have all the fun.

With raised eyebrows and a taunting head tilt Roxie asked, "You think we're friends, *Ryan?* I beg to differ." She walked past him to a row of lockers and set to working the combination dial of the one on the end.

Fig took a step back so he could see inside, but she blocked the contents with her body.

He hated the position Victoria had put him in. While he liked watching Roxie—her butt, for example, which filled out the back of her scrub pants in all of its pleasing roundness, with not one panty line—*watching* her for anything other than his own personal enjoyment felt sneaky and underhanded. Two things Fig was not.

"You see, *Ryan,* my friends don't lie to me or leave me waiting without so much as a telephone call to say that something came up or they'd received a better offer."

"I didn't…" No way she'd understand what having a mother like his was like. He didn't want to talk about that night, just wanted to put it behind him. "I'm sorry."

"Yes, *Ryan.* You are. Because you missed out on a good time."

No doubt he had. For sure he would have much rather been with her than where he'd wound up.

"Such a pity." After pushing her huge purple

purse and a lunch sack into her locker, she pulled out a hot-pink stethoscope, popped a piece of gum into her mouth and closed the door. The next thing he knew she had her chest pressed to his and was leaning in close to his ear to whisper, "I'd put on my crotchless panties and peekaboo bra especially for you."

He pulled her bottom half close. Could not stop himself. "I sure wish I'd been there to see them." And enjoy them. He drew in her sensual scent. God help him he wanted her. While Kyle liked his women small, Fig liked 'em tall and thin. Just like Roxie. He went for full body contact—skin to skin from head to toe.

At first she stood rigid, looking away from him. He slid his hands up her sides, teased the outer curve of each breast. She reacted, an infinitesimal softening, a barely noticeable exhalation, both of which he may have missed if he wasn't so attuned to her. "You want me," he observed.

"To move your hands," she replied.

He did. To her upper back where he proceeded to hug her close. Her cell phone rang.

Dag-nab-it. He released her.

She took a step back—still not looking at him—

set her stethoscope on the table and pulled out her phone to check the screen.

Fig forced himself to stop thinking about how good she'd felt pressed against him, how much he wanted to see her beautifully formed body in nothing but some sexy, barely there undergarments, and resumed focus on his mission—to determine if Roxie was the one responsible for 5E's missing Demerol. While his brain made a smooth transition, his body was not so easily redirected.

Roxie returned the phone to her pocket without answering it, and, with a deep breath, she turned and headed for the door like she'd forgotten all about him. "Hey," he called after her, holding up her stethoscope.

Seeing it, she snapped two fingers. "Right. I'll be needing that."

When she grabbed it he held on and waited for her to look him in the eye, making note that hers were bloodshot—damn. "I'm sorry you had to sit home on a Friday night because of me."

She laughed. "Don't kid yourself, *Ryan*. There are plenty of men who enjoy my company." She stared him down. "Really enjoy it. And just because you weren't up for a good time doesn't mean

I didn't have one." She yanked the stethoscope from his hand. Over her shoulder she said, "For the record, I never sit home on Friday or Saturday nights. Ever."

Her phone buzzed.

She retrieved it and looked at the screen. "I hate men." She glared at him. "I'm done with the lot of you. Every single one. So tell your kind to stay the hell away from me if they value their man-parts." Then she slammed out the door.

Fig waited, wanting a little distance between Roxie and his man-parts. At least for now. He smiled, taking her words as more of a challenge than a warning.

Roxie burst out of the lounge, her heart pounding, rage coursing through her system. She looked at the text message, again: "It's done." *"¡Coño!"* And the colossal jerk had sent her the link. She eyed the darkened hallway of even-numbered rooms, wondering if she had the strength to hurl the phone hard enough to break through the reinforced glass window at the far end. The way she felt? Probably. But what would that solve?

The video was out there for anyone with a computer to see. Her friends. Her coworkers. Her family. Of course Roxie would shrug it off, make like she didn't care. But she did. What went on in private between two consenting adults was supposed to be just that. Private. The thought of people watching, knowing, sat like a pregnant hippo on her chest.

Deep breath in. Deep breath out.

"The Lord doesn't give us more than we can handle." Roxie whispered her mantra of the past ten years and leaned her back against the wall, wishing He didn't have so much confidence in her.

Each time she thought things couldn't get worse something inevitably happened to prove her wrong. She slipped her hand into the pocket of her scrub coat and wrapped her fingers around the three cartridges of injectable Demerol. At least that she could fix before anyone found out.

Or so she'd thought until she reached the nurses' station at the center of the H-shaped unit and froze. What was Victoria doing at work so early? And why was *she* verifying the narcotic count with the night shift? The hippo gave birth to twins that landed heavily on her gut and set off a tumultuous, acidic churn. There'd be no hiding her stupidity now. Victoria was going to be livid.

"You okay?" Fig stopped beside her, standing way too close. She took the opportunity to draw on his calm and confidence to rejuvenate her dwindling supply.

"Just fine." Always fine. Fine. Fine. Fine. Roxie hoped if she said it enough it would turn out to be true.

"You're looking pale."

"We Latinos don't pale," she snapped. Not like him. Did the man ever get out in the sun? She looked up at the strong features of his handsome face and the rounded smoothness of his enticingly bald head. Actually had to look up. How often did that happen? At just under six feet, Roxie was usually the tallest person in the room. Aside from the fact she'd had a terrible day with her mom and had been really looking forward to their night out, his height played a small part in why she'd been so angry about being stood up. In search of the perfect shoes to wear on their date, actual heels, Roxie had torn through dozens of stores, had spent hours looking. Did he have any idea how difficult it'd been to find a pair of hot-pink glossy patent-leather peep-toe platform pumps? In a size thirteen? When would she ever have another opportunity to wear them?

"Hey, Rox," one of the night nurses called out from room 504. "Would you help me out? I need to get home on time today."

"Sure thing." Roxie glanced at the schedule board across from the nurses' station to confirm her assignment. District one. As usual. Even-numbered rooms 502–508. Eight beds. Two empty, awaiting new admission post-ops. One pre-op due in the operating room at 7:30 a.m. She glanced at the clock, 6:45, then turned to Fig. "When Victoria's done would you tell her I need to speak with her? It's important."

"My first official unit-clerk task." He lifted his pad and pen and wrote something down. "I'm on it."

Then Roxie got to work, assisted her colleague, took a quick report and sent her pre-op patient off to the O.R. On her morning round each of her patients had a problem. Pain. High blood pressure. Low blood pressure. Hypoglycemia. Constipation. Fever. An infiltrated IV. And two saturated dressings.

Finally, by 11:00 a.m. she had everyone settled and could take a quick break for some much-needed sustenance. Only, on her way to the nurses' lounge she met up with a recovery room nurse pushing a sleeping patient in her direction. "You're supposed to call first," Roxie said.

"I did," the plump nurse at the head of the stretcher said. "The guy who answered said to come on up."

Roxie glared at Fig. "The floor nurse gives approval to accept patients from the recovery room. Not you," she told him.

"Oops. Duly noted," Fig answered, making a note on his stupid pad. "It won't happen again."

She eyed the girth of her new patient and looked back over to Fig. "Make yourself useful. Come help us transfer this patient to her bed." May as well see if those muscles worked as good as they looked.

Fig stood, something strangely uncertain in his expression.

"No," Victoria said from behind him. "He's here as a unit clerk. The only contact he's to have with patients is from behind this desk."

What the...?

Roxie's stomach growled. She didn't have time for this nonsense. "All available hands to 502A," she called out. "Chop-chop, ladies. My blood sugar is starting to drop." That was sure to get their attention. No one wanted a cranky Roxie around.

With the recovery room nurse's help Roxie lined the stretcher up next to the bed and locked the wheels on both. "Welcome to 5E, Mrs. Flynn," she said to her new patient. "My name is Roxie Morano and I'll be your nurse until seven o'clock this evening." She raised the bed so it was the same height as the stretcher, transferred the bag of IV fluid to the bed pole and placed the catheter drainage bag by the patient's feet so it didn't pull during transfer. As the recovery room nurse gave report, Roxie checked the patient's right-sided chest dressing, which was covered by a surgical bra, and inspected the drains and tubing.

"Fifty-nine-year-old, morbidly obese female. Status post right-sided modified radical mastectomy."

Roxie noted the drainage in each of the two bulbs, labeled R1 and R2, to establish a baseline and pulled her report sheet—which contained pertinent information on each of her patients—from her pocket. She unfolded the paper and set it on the over-the-bed table. In the blank box reserved for room 502A she wrote in the patient's name and diagnosis, last set of vitals and time of last dose of pain medication. Then she jotted down her observations. Patient arousable to verbal stimuli. Catheter draining clear yellow urine. Dressing clean, dry and intact. Drains to self-suction with scant red drainage in each. IV infusing to left forearm.

When Victoria and Ali—her other best friend and the nurse working in the district next to hers—arrived to help, Roxie directed, "One on the stretcher side, one over here by me." She stood on the side of the bed, at the patient's upper body, so she'd be responsible for pulling the heaviest part of her. As her colleagues got into position Roxie spoke to her patient. "We're going to slide you onto the bed, Mrs. Flynn."

The groggy woman nodded in understanding.

"Keep your hands at your sides and let us do all the work," Roxie instructed.

Each staff member grabbed a hunk of the bottom sheet.

"Everyone ready?" Roxie locked eyes with each

woman. Just last week a patient on 4B fell between the stretcher and the bed during a transfer, suffering a severe hip fracture as a result. Not on Roxie's watch. "On my count of three. One. Two. Three."

Using every bit of strength she possessed, Roxie pulled. If the grunts around her meant anything, her coworkers were giving it all they had, too. Yet the patient barely budged.

Fig entered the room.

Victoria told him to leave.

"What kind of man would I be if I let four lovely ladies struggle when I could help?"

"Are you sure?" Victoria asked, handing him a pair of latex gloves from the box on the wall.

"Scoot over." He squeezed between Roxie and Ali, bumping Roxie's hip with his as he did. "Now tell me what to do," he said as he put on the gloves.

"Ball the sheet like this." Roxie showed him her hands. "Tight."

He took the sheet in his large hands. She remembered how they'd felt on her body, holding her just a few hours earlier, and realized how much she'd like to feel them again—and in more places. She shook her head to clear her thoughts.

"And on the count of three," she continued,

"we pull and they—" she motioned to the women on the other side of the stretcher with her chin "—push."

"Got it," Fig said, testing his grip on the sheet, looking so cute in his concentration.

"Everyone ready?" Roxie asked again and waited for each woman and Fig to respond in the affirmative. "On my count of three. One. Two. Three."

Again Roxie pulled as hard as she could, and this time the patient slid toward her like she was on plastic liner slick with baby oil.

"Wow. You *are* a strong one," Roxie said to Fig.

He smiled, a genuinely pleased smile, and winked. "Remember that." He moved closer on his way to discard his gloves in the trash can and whispered, "Dream about it."

"As if any part of you registers with my subconscious." Especially not his head—in the dream where she was a cat sleeping curled around it. Or his fair skin—in the dream where they'd lounged by a pool and she'd rubbed him with suntan lotion—repeatedly—to protect him from the harsh rays of the sun. Or his laugh, or the teasing twinkle in his green eyes, or the contagious smile that brightened his handsome face.

Something about him had made her feel safe, like she could let her guard down. Thank goodness she hadn't. He also made her want…things she didn't usually crave without a couple of beers on board. Was it his slow, laid-back demeanor and quiet confidence? His quick, dry sense of humor? His build—a perfect complement to her large frame? His distinctive look or his air of reserved power?

Whatever it was, it gave her an unsettling schoolgirl crush sort of feeling. And Roxie didn't like it. In her experience men were unreliable, opportunistic and good for one thing only—sex. Add in emotion and the fun factor took a nosedive.

"Thank you, everyone," she said.

Fig didn't move.

"Back to work, you," she said, using her hands to shoo him along. "I hear a phone ringing."

He turned his back to the patient and leaned toward her. "Your mom called," he said quietly. "She sounded upset."

Last night had been particularly difficult. Roxie hated to leave for work this morning but what else could she do? They both depended on her income.

"She said she couldn't find the knobs for the stove," he added.

Duh. Because last week she hadn't turned off a burner, which caused the macaroni and cheese she'd made to burn and spew the smoke that prompted their obnoxious, constantly complaining neighbor to call the fire department. Which was the reason every damn thing in her not-so-terrific life had gone from "barely tolerable but afloat" to "she's taking on water!" fast approaching "she's going down. Abandon ship."

"There's a perfectly logical explanation for that," Roxie said. "Which is none of your business. Next time tell her to call my cell." She turned to her patient.

Fig reached for her arm to stop her. "She told me she'd tried but you didn't answer," he whispered.

What? Roxie always answered *Mami*'s calls. She patted her breast pocket. Empty. Jammed her hands into both scrub coat pockets, rummaged through their contents. Bandage scissors. Alcohol prep pads. Tape. Three injectable Demerol cartridges. Damn it, she needed to get in to talk to Victoria. Two paperclips. Three pens. A box of thermometer probes. A roll of candies. And a breakfast bar she hadn't had time to eat.

No phone.

She yanked her hands out so fast something went flying. A pen? It rolled under the bedside stand. She'd get it later. "Shoot. Where the heck did I leave my phone?" *Mami* panicked if she couldn't reach her. How long had it been since she'd called?

Roxie bent to look under the bed.

"Hot-pink with crystals, right?" Fig asked.

"Yeah."

"I'll keep an eye out for it."

"Thanks."

"And you got these." He handed her some slips of pink paper from his pocket.

She looked at the male names on each of six message slips. So they'd seen the video. Perverts. She ripped the papers in half and tossed them in the trash. "Anything else?" she asked, losing patience, wanting to get finished admitting her patient so she could call home then find her phone. Which contained that link she should have deleted upon receipt.

"You okay?"

"I'm fine." Always fine. Fine. Fine. Fine.

After getting her new patient settled Roxie took a minute to use a phone at the nurses' station. *"Hola, Mami."*

She started to cry.

"No. Please don't cry. You don't need the stove. I left you a sandwich in the refrigerator."

"I want to make hard-boiled eggs," her mother said.

"It's egg salad. Your favorite."

"Que buena hija. You're a good daughter."

"Gracias. Look, I have to get back to work. I misplaced my phone. If you need me call the floor and Fig will get me."

Nothing.

"Okay, *Mami?"*

"Okay," she said, her mouth full. "It's good. I was hungry."

Roxie smiled. "Be careful getting back to bed. I'll come straight home after work." She hung up the phone, dropped her head and let out a sigh of relief.

When she looked up her eyes met Fig's. "If my mom calls back…"

"I'll come find you," he finished.

"Thanks." Her stomach growled.

"Go eat. If any of your patients buzz I'll have Ali or Victoria check on them."

"I think I will." She stood. Swayed. Grabbed on to the counter to steady herself at the same time Fig reached for her. "Wow. Looks like the tank is empty. Time to refuel."

"Is that all it is?" Fig asked, looking concerned. And…suspect?

"Do you have any idea how many calories it takes to run this body?" she asked. "I skipped breakfast this morning. And, thanks to you, worked through my break." She lifted a shaky hand to flatten her hair. "I'm fine." Always fine. Fine. Fine. Fine.

"I'll walk you to the lounge," Fig offered.

She pulled her elbow out of his loose hold. "Don't be ridiculous." She exited the nurses' station, her head feeling disconcertingly foggy. Maintaining focus on the lounge door, she took deep breaths, concentrated on each step and willed her body to continue moving forward. Passing out at work would not be a good thing.

Two bottles of chocolate milk and two bologna-and-cheese sandwiches on rye later, Roxie felt back to her usual self. And ready to tackle Victoria before returning to her patients.

Just outside the open door to Victoria's office, Roxie heard Fig talking. "You have your proof right there," he said. "You asked me to watch her and I did. She showed up to work with bloodshot eyes, forgot her stethoscope in the nurses' lounge and misplaced her phone—which the pharmacy tech found in the med cart."

A flush of anger heated Roxie's skin. Fig was reporting her activities to Victoria, who had asked him to watch her? Why?

"And she almost passed out at the nurses' station not fifteen minutes ago," he went on. "I think it's time to switch your focus from trying to find Roxie innocent to figuring out a way to help her out of this mess."

Find Roxie innocent of what? Help her out of what mess? Exactly how much did they know about what was going on in her life? She walked into the office and with narrowed eyes looked from Victoria—sitting behind her desk, prim and professional—to Fig, looking all relaxed in the one chair across from Victoria. "What mess might that be?" she asked Fig. "And you hired him to watch me?" she asked Victoria. "Why?"

Victoria looked down at her desk at a lone cartridge of injectable Demerol.

Roxie slid her hand into her pocket and found only two of the three that had been there earlier.

Not good.

CHAPTER TWO

ROXIE withdrew her hand from her pocket and held out what Fig assumed were the other two missing doses of Demerol in her palm. He admired her calm.

"I was planning to tell you today. I asked Fig to relay the message I needed to talk to you." She looked over at him.

He nodded.

Apparently Victoria didn't care. She looked up at Roxie. "You altered the narcotic count," she accused.

"Yes." Roxie hung her head. "But I can explain."

"You altered the narcotic count," Victoria said again. A bit louder this time. "There is no explanation to justify what you did. This is grounds for termination, you know. And there's not a thing I can do to help you. This will follow you around, Roxie. You could lose your nursing license. What were you thinking?"

"Whoa." Panic flashed in Roxie's eyes. "Can't we keep this between us?"

"No, we can't keep this between us," Victoria snapped. "Because someone or a group of some-ones have been tampering with the narcotic-distribution system in the hospital. A pharmacist identified the inaccurate count as part of a hospital-wide investigation."

That was a pretty important chunk of informa-tion she'd neglected to share.

Roxie looked ready to collapse.

Fig stood. "Here." He motioned to his chair. "Sit."

"Why, thank you," she said sarcastically, looking ready to show her appreciation by slamming him into the wall and jamming her knee into his groin. "If you'd have come to me," she hissed under her breath as she moved past him, "instead of tattling to the boss I could have fixed this."

"No, you couldn't have," Victoria said. "And don't be mad at Fig. He only did what I asked him to do."

"A rare thing, a man who does what you ask him to," Roxie said to Victoria. "Lucky me you found one."

Fig felt like the low-life informant who'd deceived a friend. Because, in essence, he had.

"Tell me what happened," Victoria said.

"Does he need to be here?" Roxie asked.

No he didn't. Fig stepped toward the door, welcoming the chance to escape.

"Yes," Victoria said. He stopped. "As an impartial witness to our conversation."

Great. There was that word *impartial* again. The more he heard it, the more he realized he wasn't impartial at all. He wanted to help Roxie, wanted to erase the anger, frustration and sadness he'd noticed in her expression since early that morning, and bring back the fun-loving woman with the beautiful smile and infectious laugh from the night they'd first met.

"Fine," Roxie said, not looking at him. "The attending suspects my patient in 508B is a malingerer probably addicted to his pain meds. He reports intractable back pain yet all his diagnostic testing since admission has been negative or within normal limits. Every time the doctor tries to change over from IM Demerol to oral pain meds, the patient balks and is on the call bell every five minutes. Mention detox and he turns irate and verbally abusive."

"I'm aware of the situation," Victoria said.

"Late Friday night the doctor ordered the patient's doses of IM Demerol to be alternated with a placebo of IM sterile normal saline. The next morning—when I came on duty—it didn't take the patient long to figure it out and demand to see the syringe before I injected him. So I kept a Demerol cartridge in my pocket to show him. Then, each time he was scheduled to receive the placebo, I switched it out at the last second. It was not easy to do, I tell you."

"And you forgot to put the Demerol back," Victoria said.

Roxie nodded. "Luckily—" she looked between him and Victoria with sad eyes "—or unluckily, as it turns out, I was assigned to narcotic count Saturday night."

"But incoming shift is supposed to count and outgoing shift records."

"I can be very persuasive when I want to be." Her lips twitched into a tiny hint of a smile. "Anyway, I knew the Demerol was in my scrub jacket, which was out at the desk at the time. I increased the number in the box of Demerol by one, planning to return it before I left. Then my mother called." Roxie let out a breath. "And I had to rush home. Sunday morning I was running late, and I bolted out of the house, leaving it safely tucked away in my dresser."

"So you altered the count again."

"What else could I do?"

"How about talk to me?" Victoria asked, her anger evident. "Warn me the count was off so I wasn't completely blindsided."

"I'm sorry. I screwed up."

"How did you wind up with the other two?" Victoria asked without acknowledging Roxie's apology.

"More of the same. I was rushing. Then they got misplaced."

"You *misplaced* three doses of Demerol?"

"No." Roxie shook her head. "Only two." Like that made it okay. "The third," she went on, "was my mistake. I'd thought it was a normal saline in my pocket, but it turned out to be a Demerol."

"What is going on with you?" Victoria yelled.

Roxie shrugged and looked down at her lap.

Both women sat in silence until Roxie asked,

"What happens now? Should I finish my shift or clean out my locker and head home?"

"Let me talk to the director and explain what happened. You returned the missing meds. Maybe..."

Fig interrupted. "Just to play devil's advocate for a second." He moved out of Roxie's reach, which was no small feat in the tiny office. "How do we know there's actual Demerol in those things and she didn't refill them with water?"

Rage flared in Roxie's eyes. She jumped up from her chair, whipped a plastic contraption from her pocket and grabbed the fluid-filled cartridges from Victoria's desk. "How about I inject all three of them into your lily-white gluteus maximus and you can vouch for their potency right before you lapse into a coma?" She inserted one of the cylinders into the injection device and took a step toward him.

"Stop it, Roxie." Tiny Victoria launched herself between them. "This isn't helping."

"But maybe it will make me feel better," she said. Then she looked at Fig. Challenging him. "You want to know for sure what's in this syringe?" She held it up, speaking slow and calm. "Drop your pants."

"The hospital is investigating medication tampering." Fig held Roxie's arms to keep her away from him. "Those cartridges left the hospital. I'm just posing the potential for substitution that any good investigator would acknowledge," he defended his question.

"He's right," Victoria agreed.

Roxie backed down and surprised him by starting to laugh. Not a happy laugh. Rather the kind of laugh that happens when things are so bad if you don't laugh you'll cry. He knew it well.

Roxie collapsed into the chair, tears streaming down her cheeks. "The irony is too much." She could barely get the words out. "I tell that idiot no." She took a deep breath, blotted her eyes with a tissue Victoria handed her and started to laugh some more. "I get blackmailed. I still say no, so he posts the video on some porn site." She laughed even harder. "And I'm accused of tampering with narcotics, and I'm getting fired, anyway." The laughing was so loud people up and down the hallway outside had to be wondering what was going on.

"Wait a minute," Fig said, remembering Roxie's phone conversation from earlier that morning. *I told you no. My answer won't change. Fine. Do what you have to do.* "Someone's blackmailing you?"

"Not anymore." The thought seemed to sober her. She inhaled deeply then exhaled as if trying to blow out any lingering giggles. "And it's all your fault." She gave him the stink eye.

What? "*My* fault?"

"If you'd have taken me out on Friday night like you were supposed to, I wouldn't have gone home with Johnny-the-jerk, who, come to find out, had his bedroom outfitted with cameras so he could videotape our little interlude."

"Who is Johnny-the-jerk?" Victoria asked.

"I'm guessing he's somehow involved with the hospital's drug tampering problem because after the deed was done—" she looked at Fig and emphasized "—*twice,* he used his tape to try to coerce me into substituting his bootlegged pills for real narcotics. He said the packaging was almost identical and no one would know. I told him *I* would know and I wouldn't do it."

"You mean you can identify him?" Victoria asked.

"I'm guessing you can, too, if you check out our video."

Victoria recoiled.

At least Fig could help with that. Computers were his thing. Audio. Video. Programing. Networking. Hacking. You name it. If there's a way to track this guy, to catch him and make him pay, Fig could do it. "Do you have the link?" he asked Roxie.

"On my cell phone, wherever that is."

Fig reached into his pocket and handed it to her. She pressed a few buttons and held up the screen to him. "May I use your computer?" he asked Victoria.

"To go to a pornography website?" She paled. "Use my laptop." She took it out of her briefcase, placed it on her desk and booted it up. Then she stood so Fig could take her chair.

He typed in the link. A few seconds later Roxie's voice called out through the speakers. "Harder," she demanded. Fig fumbled to find the volume. "Yeah, baby. That's how I like it."

Just as he'd thought, Roxie was as take-charge in the bedroom as she appeared to be in every other aspect of her life. It'd take a strong man to stay in control. Anticipation of the challenge excited him.

Until the slam of Victoria's office door reminded him where he was.

"Do you have to be so loud?" Victoria chastised Roxie.

Fig didn't mind loud as long as the volume was attached to moans and screams of delight.

"Did you honestly think I'd be quiet in the bedroom?" she asked with a hint of a playful smile.

Fig muted the computer. "Twenty-seven minutes," he commented about the length of the video, giving a nod of approval.

"Not my best night," Roxie joked.

Fig relaxed a bit.

"Almost eighty thousand views in the six hours your video's been up on this site."

"Delinquents, all of them," Roxie said, standing up and walking over to stand beside him. "What are all those people doing home during the day? Shouldn't they be working?"

"Degenerates is more like it," Victoria said, looking uncomfortable. "Can you make out the man's face?" she asked Fig.

"Five stars," he noted instead, impressed.

"I bet you're regretting standing me up on Friday night." Roxie nudged his shoulder with her hip.

More than he regretted just about anything else.

"Standing her up? You didn't tell her what happened?" Victoria asked.

"No." And Victoria had better not say anything, either.

"Tell me what?" Roxie asked.

The last thing he wanted her thinking was he was some sort of pansy mama's boy, running home every time she called. "Nothing," Fig said and flashed Victoria a "keep quiet" look.

"But…"

"Woo wee," Roxie cut Victoria off. She leaned in close to the laptop. "I look good on screen."

Yes, she did. And since she didn't seem at all upset about the video, Fig commented, too. "You have an amazing ass."

Victoria sucked in an affronted breath.

"It's one of my best features," Roxie replied proudly. She had quite a few other mighty-fine features. Fig tilted his head to get a better look at one, watched her lift her long, smooth leg. No way. She couldn't possibly… She did.

"You liking what you see?" Roxie's voice turned sexy. Alluring.

Heck yeah! But Fig thought it best not to mention how much.

As if Roxie knew, she bent close to his ear and whispered, "Then I suggest you download my video so you can watch it over and over. Because that's as close as you'll ever get to sampling my goodies, you creep."

Shut. Down.

"For heaven's sake, Roxie," Victoria said. "A man taped you having sex and loaded it onto the internet. Without your consent. And you're standing there, watching yourself as if you're okay with it. You should be outraged. Shut it off, Fig."

"And what good would my outrage do?" Roxie asked. "The video is out there. And from the number of messages I've received today, people around town have seen it. There's nothing I can do. Heck, if I can't get another nursing job, maybe I'll use it as an audition tape." She turned to Fig. "Can you make me a copy?"

"You can't be serious," Victoria said.

"I'm totally serious," Roxie said, turning somber. "You may think you know me but all you know is the part of me I allow you to see. So let me share this. At the age of fourteen I gave my virginity to the owner of the superette down the street from our home to pay off our account when my mother had no money. That may have been the first time I used my body to barter, but it certainly wasn't the last. I'm a survivor. I do what I have to do."

Based on Victoria's look of complete and utter shock, she'd had no idea. Just how close were they? Roxie's defiant stance made Fig wonder if she shared her deepest, darkest secrets with anyone.

He couldn't stand the thought of lecherous men using a young Roxie who was desperate for food. He felt sick. Yet despite her experiences she still managed to enjoy life, with a wonderful sense of humor and a vivacious spirit he envied. "The man's face is blurred out," Fig said, to change the subject.

"Trust me," Roxie said. "I know who he is. And as soon as I find him you'll know who he is, too. Tell the E.R. to be on the lookout for a white male, around five feet ten inches tall, two hundred and twenty pounds, who will be arriving most likely after midnight, sometime in the next week. If things go as planned he'll be unconscious with severe facial trauma and both testicles rammed so far up into his pelvic cavity he'll require the skilled hands of surgeon to set him back to rights."

"You need to stay away from him," Victoria urged. "He's probably dangerous."

"No more dangerous than a pissed-off Puerto Rican with a grudge. So what's your call, Vic?" Roxie stood tall. Proud. "If you're going to fire me, do it now. Otherwise I need to get back to my patients."

"Let me talk to the director," Victoria replied. "Finish out your shift. You're out on vacation for the next week due to return on Wednesday. Hopefully I'll have everything worked out by then."

"Thanks," Roxie said to Victoria. "I really am sorry about all this."

"Me, too."

After Roxie left, Victoria asked Fig, "Can you take down the video?"

"I'll need to use my own computer, but yeah. I'm sure I can."

"Do you think it's up on more than one site?"

"If it is, I'll find it."

"She's going to go after that man," Victoria said.

"I'll keep an eye on her." Fig stood. He owed her that much. "I need to get back to work, too."

"Now that we know what happened you don't have to stay on here," Victoria said.

"I know. But I'll finish out my shift."

* * *

Roxie pulled her red Scion onto the short, bumpy, part-gravel, part-concrete patch that served as her driveway, turned off the engine and leaned back in her leather seat. The tiny house she shared with *Mami* held not one good memory, and yet, rather than filling her with excitement, the prospect of being forced to live somewhere else filled her with dread—mostly because *Mami* would not handle the change well. Dull blue paint, faded, chipped black shutters—one hanging askew—and over-grown, half-dead landscaping told the world this was not a happy place. The moss growing on the roof, the saggy porch and the collection of other people's discarded stuff that overflowed into the side yard added to the dilapidated appearance.

Oh, to have her own home to return to after a hard day's work. To live a stress-free, clutter-free, mother-free existence where the only person she was responsible for was herself. To be able to open a beer, actually sit down on the living room sofa and watch some mind-numbing television.

Her cell phone rang. She dug into her huge purse on the seat beside her and looked at the screen. The hospital. She let out a breath. What did she forget? Or was it Victoria calling to tell Roxie her fate? "Hello."

"Hey," Fig said. "You ran out of here before I could give you the message from your brother."

No need to ask which one. Only Ernesto, the one closest to her in age, took the time for an occasional phone call. But, "He called the hospital?"

"No. Your cell phone. While I had it. I thought it might be your mom so I answered it."

Well, surprise, surprise. A nice gesture.

"He, uh—" Fig hesitated "—sounded angry."

What did he have to be angry about? She was the one desperately trying to reach him for over a week with no response.

"I think—" Fig hesitated again.

"Just spit it out already," Roxie said.

"I think he may have seen your video."

Not Ernesto. He'd be the last one she'd expect to…

"I'm sorry, Rox. I got tied up. I'm on my way home now, and I'll take it down as soon as I get there."

Help. From an unexpected source. "Thanks."

"You doing anything tonight?" he asked. "I thought maybe we could…"

"If I decide I need sex you're unlucky number thirteen on my list."

"I'm not calling for sex. Just dinner. I want to explain…"

Roxie noticed the bags on the front porch. "No." She sat up. "She didn't."

"What?" Fig asked.

"I've got to go." Roxie ended the call then pushed open the car door, lunged out and slammed it shut. "Not again." She stormed across the patchy grass and packed dirt of the small front yard, whipped out her key and tried to open the door. Met resistance. Shouldered it open just wide enough to squeeze through. "I told you we need to keep the doorway clear," she yelled in frustration.

Behind the door her mother had stowed five white garbage bags filled with clothes. Roxie picked each up and hurled them, one at a time, into the depths of what used to be the family room, bringing the junk piled in the far corner up to chest level.

"This is crazy!" Roxie screamed. "Why are the bags back on the porch?" Two huge black garbage bags, filled to capacity, put out at the curb for the sanitation service to pick up that morning.

Two bags of trash that were no longer adding to the safety hazards of their home. A mere speck of progress in cleaning out the house. Derailed. "And I told you to stop accepting used clothing from the church." A total of five bags that she saw. But who knew if her mother had more stashed somewhere?

"*Deja de gritar.* Stop yelling," *Mami* said, shuffling slowly, carefully along the narrow pathway from the back of the house to the kitchen, the clutter on either side of her hip-high.

"Do you understand what happens if the fire marshal doesn't see a noticeable improvement in our living conditions? He'll condemn this house as unfit for human habitation. If we don't sort through this junk—like I've been trying to get you to do for years—he's going to do it. We'll be forced to leave. I can't afford a mortgage payment and a rent payment. We have one lousy week left. One week." An impossible time frame to sort through years of accumulation. The two bags she'd managed to drag to the curb had taken at least a dozen hours of encouragement and convincing to get her mother to part with her treasured possessions. And now, not only were they back, but she'd accepted five more.

"I won't leave my house." Her mother stood tall

despite her slightly hunched shoulders, looked vaguely formidable despite her frailty and washed-out floral housedress. "These are my things. *Tus hermanos vendrán.* Your brothers will come. You'll see."

Not one of her four brothers had visited "the den of crazy" in the fifteen years since the last one had moved out, leaving Roxie—her mother's unsuccessful attempt to save her failing marriage—to care for her mother, the house and herself, on her own, since the age of ten.

"If they think it's unsafe for you to go on living here—" and what normal person wouldn't? "—they will *make* you leave." The interior looked like a huge refuse heap, with only the tops of long-standing, partially collapsed piles available to view. Children's clothes, toys, magazines and books—for the grandchildren her mother had never met. Housewares—for the daughters-in-law who shunned her. Newspapers—to wrap the castaway finds for safe transport when her sons returned home to finally accept their *mami*'s gifts of love.

Too little. Too late.

And while the brothers, who'd never had time for their way-younger sister, continued to rebel against the past and focus on their futures, Roxie lived an ant-farm existence, maneuvering along paths she maintained daily, leading from the front door to the kitchen, two of the three bedrooms and the bathroom. Seven years ago she'd closed the door to the third bedroom—so cluttered with junk it was unsafe to enter—and to her knowledge, the door hadn't been opened since.

"They'll physically remove you, *Mami.*" When she refused and fought, like Roxie knew she would, what then? Would she get hurt? Have a heart attack? Get a free trip to the psych ward over at Madrin Memorial?

Maybe that's what she needed. Maybe the firemen alerting the fire marshal and health department to the state of their home was exactly what *Mami* needed to finally deal with her hoarding and allow Roxie to clean more than the bathroom and kitchen counters.

"Lo siento," *Mami* said, wringing her hands. "I'm sorry. But I couldn't find the stuffed frog for little Daniel. I thought maybe it was in one of the trash bags."

"It's in the dryer," Roxie said. "It needed to be washed. Remember?"

Mami looked down at her hands.

No. She didn't remember. Which was another reason Roxie needed to clean out the house. If *Mami*'s health continued to deteriorate, soon she'd need someone to supervise her while Roxie was at work. Whereever she happened to be working. If she was working.

She had to work. And she'd need a good job to continue to support the two of them and pay for the house and an attendant and the cleaning crew she'd put off hiring, worried the stress of strangers in their home would be too much for *Mami*.

But they were running out of time. "*Mami*. We need help. We can't do this on our own," she broached the topic. "There's a..."

"*No.*"

"Please. Be reasonable." It was the same argument every time. "We can't continue to live like this." Existing was more like it. *Mami* had no friends except for some women from the church, a bunch of enablers who inventoried the donated items and contacted her to see what she "needed."

Roxie couldn't entertain, spent the hours at home confined to her bedroom—the only clean, orderly room in the house because she dead-bolted the door whenever she left—unless she was supervising her mom's shower, cajoling her to sort and clean or cooking the meals they ate on wooden TV trays surrounded by Roxie's hepa filters which just barely neutralized the odor of decay, and God knew what else, that lingered outside her door.

"Lo siento," *Mami* said again, this time with a sniffle. "I'm sorry."

Great. Roxie felt like a big bully. She'd made her mother cry. She stepped over a small stack of magazines and skirted around a laundry basket that held dozens of her mom's favorite frogs to reach her. "I'm sorry, too." For yelling, for forgetting, albeit momentarily, that hoarding was a mental illness and not laziness or purposeful behavior meant to upset Roxie. She pulled the only family member who really mattered to her into a hug. "It'll all work out, *Mami*." Although how it would, she had no idea.

"I'll do better," *Mami* said. "After dinner. We can try again."

It was always later or tomorrow. Any time but right now.

"We can do it. We don't need a bunch of strangers in here." *Mami* scanned the devastation that had once been a large eat-in kitchen, family room and dining room, and sighed. "It's overwhelming."

"One area at a time," Roxie said, taking *Mami*'s hand and leading her along the path through the kitchen. "You decide, like on the television show. We'll continue with our piles. One for each of the boys and their families. And one for...*Papi*." She nearly choked on the word. "But you'll have to let me box it all up and mail it."

"No. They need to come. I want to see them to show them."

They weren't going to come. *Mami*'s ex-husband—who Roxie referred to as such because he refused to accept she was his daughter—had remarried years ago. As for her brothers, the only one she had any semblance of a relationship with was Ernesto—if you considered an annual birth-day telephone call and occasional requests for money a relationship—and he hadn't come home any of the other times she'd asked him to, so she didn't hold out much hope he'd suddenly devel-oped a conscience.

"Let's eat," Roxie said, changing the subject. She'd had about all the confrontation she could handle for one day.

Despite her moratorium on men, by Thursday night, forced by the frustration of *Mami* refusing to clean and annoyance at the number and tone of the messages piling up on her cell phone in relation to her video, the neon-pink and fluorescent-orange walls of Roxie's bedroom seemed to squeeze in on her. And under the weight of worry about where they'd go when forced to leave their home and what would happen if she lost her job, her bright sunshine-yellow ceiling seemed to sag until she felt it just might smother her. Roxie needed to get out, to mingle and occupy her mind so she'd stop obsessing about things outside of her control.

"Shake it off." Roxie shook out her arms and legs then rotated her neck. "Nothing you can do about it." Play it cool. She slid each foot into a flat gold-colored sandal that showed off her bright pink self-manicured toenails to perfection. "Nothing bothers Roxie Morano." She walked over to the dresser and inserted a large gold hoop earring into each earlobe. Then she stood tall and evaluated her reflection in the full-length mirror angled high on her wall.

Denim mini hugging tight to her curves. She swiveled to get a look at her butt. Check.

Legs smooth and lotioned to an enticing sheen. Check.

Hair a mass of loose, wild curls lending a care-free, untamed appearance. Check.

Tube top—in an attention-getting hot-pink—accentuating each of her womanly assets. Check and check.

Roxie was ready to go. A quick peek to make sure her mother was sleeping, and she went out-side to wait for the cab, antsy to get find-the-humor-in-anything drunk, psyched to lose herself in some make-me-forget-how-much-my-life-sucks-at-the-moment sex. Preferably of the un-videotaped variety.

Outside the heavy wooden doors to O'Halloran's Bar, one of three bars in town, and the preferred drinking and bar food eating establishment for the majority of Madrin Memorial employees, Roxie hesitated. While the music from the jukebox beck-oned her, she sought fortification in the vibration of the bass and swayed her hips to the slow rhyth-mic beat.

She could do this. So what if the people inside had watched her video, had seen her naked and wild with passion? At least they hadn't seen the worst of it. She let out a breath, determined to enjoy this night. Tomorrow she'd deal with Johnny's new threat.

"You don't have to go in there," a male voice said from behind her.

For a split second she stiffened, until she recognized it as Fig's voice.

"We can go someplace else. Maybe talk a bit more about what we're going to do to each other when we get naked."

Like they'd passed the time at the employee recognition dinner last week. "You see that's where we differ." She turned and gave him the once-over, noting his loose-fitting, expensive-looking jeans, long-sleeve white tee, black leather vest and black ascot cap. Damn it if he didn't smell even better than he looked. "I like the doing more than I like the talking." She reached for the handle on the door. "And I'm not one to hide out because of a little controversy."

"Then allow me." He pushed one hand past hers and opened the door. The other he set at her low back and, applying a gentle pressure, eased her inside.

Just as the song on the jukebox ended. The bar went quiet. All eyes turned on her. Roxie hesitated.

Fig leaned in close, his chest pressed to her back, his palm flat on her belly. "Time to muster up some moxie, Roxie," he whispered. "Every woman in this bar is wishing she had a body as gorgeous as yours, and every man is wishing he had your long, beautiful legs clamped around his butt."

Roxie relaxed. Smiled even. "Does that include you?" She allowed herself to be led to the large wooden bar.

"Nah." He assisted her up onto a stool, even though she didn't need assistance then slid onto the stool beside her. He looked up, locked a pair of dreamy green eyes with hers and added, "My wish involves them wrapped around my head."

Hell-o! An excited tingle started—there—and flared out to her periphery. Roxie came danger-ously close to grabbing him by the arm and drag-ging him off to someplace more private. So she could grant a little wish fulfillment. Because with men there was a Polly Pocket–size window of op-portunity between "I want to make you feel so good" and "me, me, me." But, "So that's why you're here? Sex?" Making him no better than the rest of her post-pornographic-video fan club. Too busy to bother with an official date, too cheap to shell out some bucks on dinner and a movie, but ready to get naked at the first opportunity. The slug.

"I'm here because Victoria's worried you're heading down a dangerous path."

"Ah. How sweet." Not. "And she sent her does-what-he's-asked-to-do lackey to stop me?" Roxie stood. "Well, thanks anyway, but I don't need a keeper." She didn't need anyone.

"I beg to differ." He caught her by a belt loop on her skirt as she tried to walk away. "Sit down," he said quietly, but it was an order all the same.

Not likely. "Who do you think…?"

"I can tie a cherry stem in a knot using only my tongue and teeth," he said, calm as can be. The randomness of his comment caught her off guard. Intrigued, Roxie stopped.

"In eight seconds," he added with a slow, confident smile.

He was too cocky for his own good. "Triple B," she called the bartender. "The usual for me. My friend would like something with a cherry in it."

"I guess that leaves you out," Raunchy Rob from Radiology called from the other side of the bar. The guy next to him laughed.

"Ha-ha," Roxie said. Idiot.

Fig stood, looking ready to do some damage. "Apologize to the lady," he demanded.

"What?" Rob asked. "I was only having some fun. You know I love you, Roxie." He snickered. "Even more so on my computer screen." He elbowed the loser next to him. They both chuckled.

Fig took off.

Now it was Roxie holding *him* by the belt loop in a futile attempt to slow him down. "Don't." The man was a plow horse. She was the plow, her sandals absolutely no help in the traction department. "Oh, look," she tried. "Our drinks. Time to prove your oral dexterity." Fig kept on going. "For heaven's sake, apologize, Rob. Or I'll tell everyone…" about his stubby little pecker. What a miserable night that'd been.

"I'm sorry." Rob hopped off his stool and backed across the dance floor. "I'm sorry. Hell, Roxie. Call him off."

CHAPTER THREE

FLIRTY banter and sarcastic teasing aside, Fig refused to stand by and do nothing when a poor excuse for a man flat-out disrespected a lady. Especially one he considered a friend, whether or not she considered him a friend in return. When the loud mouth pleaded out an apology then scurried away, Fig stopped. "Anyone else have anything to say?" he asked the now quiet crowd. He stood tall, his arms at his sides, prepared to fight, hoping he didn't have to.

Because he had plans for later tonight and they didn't include a visit to the emergency room.

No one spoke.

Good.

Gradually the bar's patrons resumed their conversations and turned back to their pool and dart games. Time to take Roxie's mind off her quest for vengeance and convince her to leave. With him.

"My hero," Roxie teased from beside him.

She looked down at the wood floor and nudged a small drink umbrella with the toe of her delicate gold sandal. "But if you're looking to protect my honor, I'm afraid you're at least ten years too late. I've had sex with—" she scanned the crowd "—at least half the men in here tonight. I bet the other half have watched me doing the videotaped hoochie coochie probably with their hands down their pants." She shrugged. "I'm not proud of it. But I'm not ashamed, either. It is what it is. I am who I am."

He appreciated her honesty. "I like who you are."

She smiled up at him. "Because you want me to wrap my legs around your head."

"Hey. Don't knock it." He matched her grin. "I'll make sure you enjoy yourself as much as I do." Turned out Fig had a real knack for pleasuring women. He may have hit the sex scene later than most, but according to several very reliable sources he'd surpassed the competition in the oral sex arena.

Two positives to come out of months and months spent as a patient in the hospital:

Patience. From waiting for the nurses to bring his medication, waiting to get strong enough to walk to the bathroom on his own, to get healthy enough to return home. Women seemed to like his unhurried approach to foreplay.

Chivalry. From the hours and hours of black-and-white classic movies his mother watched at his bedside. When he'd pretended to be asleep so she'd stop fussing over him. When he'd vowed if he survived long enough, got big and strong and lucky enough to find a woman who didn't think he was a sickly, hairless freak, he'd treat her like a princess. In his early twenties he'd learned as much as they touted equality, women liked to be treated special, to be protected, cared for and respected. As much as they wanted independence, they liked a man to take charge.

With that thought in mind, Fig caught Roxie around the waist, pulled her close. "Dance with me."

Roxie settled her body flush with his and clasped her hands behind his neck. "Since you *asked* so nicely."

Fig rested his hands on her hips, his cheek to her mane of soft, lightly perfumed curls, and swayed in time with the slow beat, loving the closeness, the feel of her. But he needed Roxie to understand. "About our date."

She leaned back to look at him. "You mean the one I got all dressed up for? The one I'd been looking forward to all week? The one you didn't bother to show up for?"

"That's the one." He pulled her back against his body and held her there. "I had a family emergency and had to run home for the weekend. Can we leave it at that as long as you know I didn't get a better offer, because there's no place I would have rather been than with you that night? And if there was any way I could have gotten to you I would have? I should have called." But he'd been enraged that his mother had manipulated him. Again. For the absolute last time. "I'm sorry."

"And…" Roxie said.

"I'm sorry for what went down at the hospital. I had no idea the investigation was hospital wide. Victoria asked me to help prove your innocence, and that's what I'd intended to do."

"A-a-and?"

And what? Fig had no idea.

"And you're going to make it up to me."

"Yes." Most definitely. "And I'm going to make

it up to you." Tonight. All night long. Fig slid his hands into her back pockets and eased her hips closer, putting her in contact with his growing arousal, making his intentions clear. They'd had quite a tempting flirtation going last weekend, and Fig was eager to back up his words with a little action.

Roxie turned her head, her mouth on his ear, her breath warm and moist. "By taking off your cap so I can feel your head."

The head wearing the hat was not the head he wanted her hands on at the moment. He leaned back so he could face her. "You want to…"

She nodded. "Feel your head," she said, looking up at him. "It looks so soft."

What was it with women and a bald-headed men? Far from being the turn-off he'd once thought it to be, they loved it, asked to caress it and pet it. Holding Roxie in place with his left arm at her low back, Fig pulled off his cap. Holding it, his right hand joined his left and he said, "Feel away."

She slid both hands up the back of his neck to the top of his head. For as loud and in-your-face as Roxie could be, she had a gentle touch, skimming lightly across his flesh. Fig wanted to bury his face in her hair, close his eyes and enjoy every second of it.

Total loser that he was, a simple caress from Roxie was capable of turning him to mush. Like on his twenty-first birthday, when he'd undressed Kyle's gift—one of the always-looking-for-a-good-time Stavardi twins—and almost didn't last long enough to lose his virginity. Luckily he'd had enough presence of mind to put his mentor's sage advice into action: take control. Focus on the woman. Always satisfy your partner—multiple times when possible—before allowing yourself to come. That last one had taken some time to master. But he was nothing if not a good student, committed and willing to practice, often, until he'd gotten it right. After a few months his confidence grew and word got around and he'd never again needed Kyle's help to attract women.

Fig slid his hands back into the pockets covering Roxie's nicely rounded butt. He'd already taken control. Now he'd focus on the woman. "Nice," he said.

"Yeah," she muttered on a sigh, her hands still exploring. "Soooo, is the rest of you this enticingly smooth and hair-free?" she asked.

He smiled. "If you're a really good girl maybe you'll get to find out," he teased.

"Oh, I'm good."

From the snippet of her video he'd watched in Victoria's office, he'd lay odds she was much better than good. His cell phone vibrated in his front pocket.

Roxie rubbed against it. "Me likey."

"You're a kook," he joked, ignoring the call. Less than a minute later, it vibrated again. His mother's typical pattern. Call incessantly until he picked up. Call the local police if he didn't answer within an hour.

Tomorrow he'd get a new number.

"You'd better answer that," Roxie said when the phone buzzed a third time. "Not that I'm not enjoying all the activity down there, but it may be important."

He reached into his pocket to retrieve his phone and checked the caller. Sure enough. Still holding Roxie, he answered the call. "Hi, Mom. I'm fine. Goodbye," he said. And put the phone away.

It buzzed again.

"Talk to your mom," Roxie said, starting to pull away.

"I'm not ready to let you go." Fig held on. "We were in the middle of discussing how good you are." A topic he'd like to address in detail as a prelude to the demonstration portion of the evening.

"Our drinks are getting warm." She pushed on his chest and he released her. "I promise to save you a dance for later."

Save him a dance? He intended to have all of her dances. Back at the bar an open bottle of beer and three shot glasses filled with a dark amber liquid awaited Roxie. A Shirley Temple with a long-stemmed maraschino cherry awaited him.

Fig reached under the bar, squirted a dollop of hand sanitizer in his palm and cleaned his hands. That done, he removed the stem from the cherry—regretting having mentioned his unusual skill—and wiped it with his napkin. He lifted the glass, toasted the bartender, who smiled, and returned it to the bar without taking a sip. Last night they'd joked around for a couple of hours while Fig had waited to see if Roxie would show up. After serving Fig his third bottle of water—unopened—the bartender had offered him a shot of anything, on the house. Fig had refused and shared he no longer drank alcohol—thus the Shirley Temple.

He'd tried living life under an alcoholic haze through which his situation passed as acceptable. As a result the abuse had gone on years longer than it should have. Because he wasn't clearheaded enough to notice it. Because it took Kyle almost dying for him to figure it out.

Roxie tossed back a shot.

The bartender, who she called Triple B—for Big Burly Bartender—came over to tell her which man had purchased each shot for her. And to bring Fig a bottle of water—unopened.

Roxie looked at it with disgust. "You want one?" She held up a shot glass.

"No. I'm good."

She tossed back the second one.

Fig recognized Roxie's need to get drunk. Fast. More to escape and forget than embark on a little giddy, uninhibited fun. Been there, done that. "Did you drive tonight?"

"Nah." She followed the shot with a swig of beer. Then smiled. "I'm sure someone will be willing to give me a ride home."

When alcohol rendered her inhibitions ineffective. "I'll drive you home," he said. Even if he had to drag her out by her hair while swinging Triple

B's behind-the-bar baseball bat back and forth to hold off the predators.

She lifted her third shot, smiled at some blond-haired schlub who blew her a kiss and finished that one off. "Don't you dare ruin my fun, figlet. Go call your mother."

Figlet. His man-parts shriveled in response. Roxie turned to face the man sitting on the other side of her and began to chat, effectively dismissing him. He took the opportunity to dial his mom. When she picked up he said, "I'm fine, Mom. Now's not a good time to talk. I'll call you tomorrow."

He caught Roxie watching him out of the corner of her eye. "I'm on a date," he answered when his mom shot off a question about why it was so noisy.

"Oh, you think this is a date?" Roxie asked, her head tilted to the side and both eyebrows raised.

He smiled. "No. She's not a nice Jewish girl," he answered his mom.

Roxie harrumphed and brought her bottle of beer to her lips.

"She's a nice Latina girl," he clarified.

She smiled around the opening.

"Yes. They do have beautiful complexions."

He drew a figure eight on the warm, bare skin of Roxie's upper back. She shivered.

"Okay, Mom," Fig said when she told him to be careful.

"Always," he agreed when she told him to use protection.

"Never," he denied when she reminded him not to kiss his date on the mouth—because the human mouth was the dirtiest part of the body and kissing transmitted disease.

And, "I will," he agreed when she told him to have fun (but not too much), get a good night's sleep (after he got rid of the shiksa) and to call her tomorrow (so she'd know he'd survived the night). He disconnected the call without saying what needed to be said. That he was twenty-six years old and she needed to find a hobby or something else to occupy her time.

To which she would have replied, "You can't turn off being a mother, Ryan. Especially to a sick son who you've given up your own life to care for and homeschool." Certain he would have given up his own life if not for his mom's steadfast love and encouragement when he was young, Fig indulged her. He'd even forgiven her. But he'd reached his limit of guilt and manipulation. If they were going to have any type of relationship from here on, it'd be on his terms. Which he planned to lay out for her the next time they met face-to-face. Not in a bar, with Roxie listening in.

"Your mom sounded disappointed that you're hanging out with a shiksa. Good luck finding a nice Jewish girl here at O'Halloran's. Don't look so surprised." Roxie shrugged and looked down into her third shot glass. "Mom and I used to clean for a Jewish family up on the hill. I heard what they said."

"Maybe I don't want a nice Jewish girl," Fig said, leaning in, trying to make eye contact.

She bumped him with her shoulder. "You and me are like matzo balls and hot sauce. We don't mix."

Fig disagreed. The potent chemistry he and Roxie shared was a perfect mix. "What do you know about matzo balls?"

"Sometimes we helped Mrs. Klein prepare and serve at Rosh Hashanah and Passover. I'll have you know I can make a chicken soup so tasty and a matzo ball so light and fluffy your mom would weep."

"Maybe I like my matzo balls as hot and spicy as I like my women."

This time Roxie laughed. "I'm out of your league."

"Maybe this will change your mind." Fig lifted the cherry stem and held out his expensive watch. "Time me."

She counted him down. "Five. Four…"

He placed the stem between his teeth.

"One," Roxie said and stared at his lips.

Fig maneuvered the stem with his tongue. Twisted it, shoved it and…*voilà!* He spit the knotted stem into his palm.

Roxie looked down at the watch. And swallowed. "Eight seconds."

He leaned in close. "Imagine what a few minutes of that would feel like." Her expression softened. Ah, yes. He had her. Atta girl. Imagine him going down…

The tall man with blond hair came up beside Roxie. "Come on, hot stuff," he said, grabbing her arm. "They're playing our song."

"Born to be Wild."

Roxie looked torn—for all of five seconds. "Go home," she said. "I'll tell Victoria you did your best." Then she hopped off her stool and led scruffy surfer dude to the dance floor.

As if Victoria's concern was the only reason he'd come to the bar.

"She's headed for trouble with that one," Triple B commented. "Even more than with the last loser she paired herself off with."

Fig stiffened. "The last loser." The videographer. "You know him? What he did?"

Triple B nodded as he picked up a glass and started drying it with a towel. "He started coming in a few weeks ago. Always after midnight." He set down the glass and picked up another. "Him and a shifty-looking sidekick. They moved through the crowd. Zeroed in on a certain woman and started buying rounds of drinks until they practically had to carry her out." He slammed the glass on the bar. "What could I do? The women didn't protest. They didn't ask for help. The next time they come in here…"

"You call *me,*" Fig said. He removed his business card from his wallet and handed it to the bartender. "Anytime."

For the next hour Fig listened to an increasingly loud, slurring, laughing Roxie sing—if you could call it that—along with the jukebox. He watched the enticing gyration of her hips and the bounce of her pleasing breasts as she danced and stumbled from one groping partner to the next, only resting long enough to do a shot or chug down a constant supply of beer, a fresh drink purchased by her many admirers before she'd completely finished the one before it. He kept an eye on the time and waited for the right opportunity to claim the dance she'd promised him so he could entice her away from the bar. Before midnight.

It happened in an instant. Roxie pushed the blond guy away. Fig made it to the dance floor just in time to hear him say, "Come on, baby. Double your pleasure," as he threaded his right arm through Roxie's, and another man, who could have passed for his twin, did the same on the other side. Their execution practiced. Effective. They led Roxie to the door.

"I don't do tag team, fellas," Roxie said, looking at each. "If you don't…"

"A real man doesn't need help to pleasure a woman," Fig said, coming to a stop directly in front of Roxie. The men halted. Roxie didn't.

"Right on, figlet," she said just before she collided with his chest.

He caught her and held her upright as he leaned in close to her ear. "There are two of them and only one of me. It'd help if you talked me up, not down."

She stepped back. "I mean, Big Fig," she corrected. "Big *Bad* Fig," she emphasized. It would have been more effective if her tone had been less mocking.

"How about that dance?" he asked, holding out his hand. Cautious. Not sure how the duo once again flanking Roxie would respond.

"Ta ta." She dismissed them with a flippant wave. "It's been fun."

"I don't think so," one said at the same time the other said, "Not after all the money…"

"Triple B," Fig called out to the bartender. "Add their tab to mine." He motioned between the two men. "If they make their way back to the bar in the next ten seconds, tack on whatever they drink for the rest of the night." He turned to both men. "It's the only offer on the table, gentlemen." He pushed back his shoulders and widened his stance. "The lady's with me."

"How absolutely caveman of you," Roxie said with a grin. "I think I like it."

They all did.

The scruffier of the two men looked Fig up and down. Fig had about six inches on him. With a curse he returned to the bar. After a brief hesitation, the other one followed.

"Come on." He held open his arms. "You promised me a dance."

The music playing had a raucous beat.

"I'm tired," Roxie admitted.

"Too tired for a slow dance?"

She swayed on her feet. "I'm all hot and sweaty," she said.

Fig closed the distance between them and pulled her close. "Next time I want to be the one to make you all hot and sweaty."

She rested her head on his shoulder and followed his lead, leaning heavily. "I like that idea," she said as her hands snaked up his arms and the back of his neck, coming to rest on his head. "Nice," she said on an exhalation as she caressed him.

Nice indeed.

After the second song Fig thought there was a distinct possibility Roxie had fallen asleep. "Hey," he said, rubbing her back. "I'm going to take you home now."

"To *your* home."

Well, Kyle's condo since it was where Fig was staying while in town since Kyle had all but moved in with Victoria. That'd been the plan, anyway. Before he'd seen Roxie consume enough alcohol to fell a lumberjack. The first time he hankied her panky he wanted her fully alert, capable of consent and of remembering their encounter—so she'd stop calling him figlet.

Unlike his lesser male counterparts, Fig did not take advantage of intoxicated women.

"Come on, hot sauce," he said, giving no indication he'd be taking her directly home to her house. It was eleven forty-four and he didn't have time for an argument.

"Sure thing, matzo ball," she said with a giggle. "You know you kind of look like a matzo ball."

"Is that your idea of a compliment?" he asked, leading her to the bar so he could settle up with Triple B and get his cap.

"I like matzo balls," she said defensively.

At least that was a start.

* * *

During the walk across the parking lot, the fresh air rejuvenated Roxie. Made her ache with want. Excitement started to build. For sex. For a wipe-my-mind-clean orgasm and the blessed satiated calm that followed.

After all of Fig's big talk last week, he had better deliver.

Uh-oh. "You know what they say about men and expensive sports cars," Roxie said when he brought her to an uber-fancy silver Corvette.

He spun her around so fast her head kept going. Before she knew what'd happened he had her pinned to the side of said fancy sports car. Then he grabbed her ass, lifted her left leg behind the knee and ground his zipper against the dampening cotton lining of her undies. "Ya know…" he said.

If Roxie were a smidgen less intoxicated and a bit more coordinated she would have jumped up, wrapped her other leg around him and hung there. His yin to her yang.

"…one day soon," he continued, "you are going to owe me a huge—" he held her tight and ground his erection against the very place she wanted him "—and when I say huge I mean *huge*—apology."

Before she could make sense of the "someday

soon" time frame, he pulled away, opened the door and helped her in. "I feel like my butt's dragging on the ground," she said when he pulled onto the open road.

"Close your eyes," he suggested.

She did and felt the car accelerate. The power. The speed. She loved it. Until the car started to spin. Bad idea. She opened them back up and focused in on the hula girl on the dashboard.

"You okay?" Fig asked. The electric window to her right opened. The cool night air blew through her hair. She felt wild and free. And gassy. She burped. Her attempt to quickly cover her mouth wound up an awkward smack in the nose. "Sorry." She waited for his censure, for his condemnation for how drunk she was.

Instead he burped, too. "Now *that* feels better," he said.

Smiling, Roxie relaxed into the welcoming soft leather seat. Until she noticed they were headed toward her house, not Kyle's condo. "Hey," she said. "We're supposed to be going to your place." To rip each other's clothes off. To have sex like wild wildebeests out on the Serengeti. "So you'd best pull a U-ey and get us going in the right direction." She hoped the walls of Kyle's condo had sufficient soundproofing between his unit and the ones next door.

"I'm taking you home, Roxie. To your house."

"Oh, hell no." Roxie sat up. "I have until three."

She could see Fig's smile in the light from the speedometer. "What happens to you at three?"

Mami started prowling around. Roxie's brief opportunity to play at carefreeness ended and she returned to her hellish existence inside the walls of the childhood home she hated.

"I am *muy caliente* for you, figlet," she tried, leaning across the center console to slip her tongue in his ear while she ran her hand from his knee up the inside of his thigh.

He covered her hand with his and stopped her, mere inches from her destination. "What's with the figlet?" he asked, moving her hand to her own thigh. "You keep calling me that and I doubt I'll get turned on enough to put out the flame atop a birthday candle much less take on the blaze you've got going."

"Fine." Roxie crossed her arms over her chest and stared out the window. "If we're not going to have sex then take me back to the bar," she said, feeling tense from a potent mix of anger, frustration and lust churning inside her.

"Why?" Fig asked. "So you can find someone else to screw you?"

He made it sound immoral. "What's wrong with two people having sex? Finding enjoyment and satisfaction in each other's bodies?"

"That's exactly the reason we're not going to have sex tonight," he said, sounding a little pissed off himself. "When we're together—and notice I say *when* not *if*—" he glanced at her then looked back at the road "—it will be because we both want each other, not because any member of the opposite sex will do."

And to Roxie's utter disgust she started to cry. "How could you do this to me?" she wailed. "You have no idea…" she sobbed. "I need…"

"I know what you need, honey," he said, placing his cool palm on her thigh. "When I get you settled into your bed I'll take care of you."

If the thought of him seeing the inside of her home hadn't sent her into a panic, she may have had more time to think about how sweet he sounded just then. "You are not coming into my house." She wiped at her wet eyes with the back of her hand.

"I don't want you anywhere near my house." She reached for the handle to open the car door. "Let me out here." She tried to yank on it.

Fig slammed on the brakes and grabbed her hand. "Are you insane?" He swerved the car onto the shoulder of the road.

"Why can't anything go the way I want it to?" She fought Fig. "Why do you do what Victoria asks and not what I ask?" She opened the door, hauled herself out and screamed up at the starless sky. "Is one night of fun too much to ask for? One freakin' night?" She turned and pounded toward her house.

"Where are you going?" Fig asked.

As if it weren't clear by the direction she was headed. "Home," she snapped. "That's where you want me to go, right? So that's where I'm going. To *my* home. Where *you* are not welcome," she screamed. "Good. Night." Although why she'd wished him a good night when hers was getting suckier by the second—because of him—was a mystery. May his tire pick up a nail on the way home and he be greeted with a flat first thing in the morning. Four flats. "If you won't do it for me," she yelled at the sky, "do it because he deserves it."

"Who deserves what?" Fig jogged after her.

"You'd better not leave your precious car unattended in this neighborhood. You'll come back to find all your tires missing."

That'll do, Roxie thought as she turned the corner onto her road. The darkness enveloped her. She'd walked this route hundreds of times, didn't need light to see where she was going. Unfortunately Fig didn't know enough to step over the hose Mr. Victor kept laid out across the sidewalk to drain his sump pump into the sewer grate.

"Damn it," Fig said in the midst of trying to keep himself from falling to the ground.

Roxie smiled, wishing she could have seen it.

"Any more hazards I should be aware of?" he asked from beside her.

"I think I heard the sound of your windshield shattering. Probably vandals. You'd better go check it out."

"It's only a car. It can be replaced."

Roxie stopped short. Fig bumped into her. Three more houses and she'd be home. It was time to put an end to this nonsense. "See that light up ahead? That's my house. I am certain I can make it there unassisted." Because her anger had sobered her up but good.

"I don't mind walking you." He took her arm in his.

Daring man. "Well, I mind." She yanked herself free.

"Let me take you out tomorrow," Fig said. "Or better yet, come to my place. I'll cook you a delicious meal. Tell me what you like. I'm up for anything."

"I choose O'Halloran's. Without you. So I can get drunk and go home with someone who's up to the task of giving me what I want."

"Oh, I'll give you what you want and more," Fig said. "When you're sober."

"Sex is more fun when I'm drunk." Which worked for her, since that's the only time she ever wanted it. Until she'd met Fig.

He turned to her, his face so close she felt his breath on her cheek. "Then you're not doing it with the right men."

Her phone rang. She pulled it out of the front pocket of her skirt and looked at the lit display. *Mami*. She whipped it open. "What's wrong?" It was just after midnight. *Mami* always slept until at least 3:00 a.m.

"I smell smoke," *Mami* said, coughing.

Roxie sniffed the air.

And ran.

Her sandals slapped the broken-up sidewalk. The bottoms of her feet stung. She didn't stop. This was all her fault. The fire marshal had warned the house was unsafe. A fire hazard. But *Mami* had clutched at her chest and grabbed for her sublingual nitroglycerin tablets when Roxie broached the subject of living someplace else, even temporarily.

Fig called out behind her.

Roxie didn't answer. She should have done more, tried harder. Now *Mami* would pay the price for her failure. She tore up the front lawn. Thick, dark gray smoke billowed from the open kitchen window. Roxie jammed her hand in her front pocket to get her key and took the front steps all three at once.

"Wait," Fig yelled.

Roxie inserted the key in the lock.

Fig tackled her. "I said wait."

"My mother's in there," Roxie yelled. "Get off of me." She struggled beneath him.

He tightened his hold. "I called the fire department. They'll be here in a minute."

But they wouldn't be able to locate her amongst

the clutter. Only Roxie knew the path to the back bedroom, what she needed to skirt around and climb over. Only Roxie knew where *Mami* would be, huddled near the edge of her mattress, her bed all but taken over by dolls and clothing she worked to repair, and beloved mementos of her life with her husband.

"You don't understand." She fought with every bit of strength she had and managed to turn onto her back.

"Stop it," Fig said. "You're going to hurt yourself."

Roxie didn't care about herself. Tears leaked from her eyes. "Only I can get to her. I have to get her."

"You're not thinking clearly."

She was thinking clearly enough to know he was stronger than her and had the advantage of being on top of her, and the only thing she could do to escape him was knee him in the balls as soon as the opportunity presented itself.

Which is what she did.

Fig sucked in a breath and forgot about her for the few seconds it took to push him away. She felt a moment's remorse at the sight of him lying on his side in the fetal position, before she opened the door.

A huge blast of heat and smoke greeted her. When it dissipated she yelled, "*Mami,* I'm coming." Then she headed into the darkness.

CHAPTER FOUR

"ARE you insane?" Fig yelled at Roxie for the second time that night as she removed the oxygen mask, again, and coughed. Black soot stained her face—especially beneath her nostrils—and clothes. "You could have been killed."

While he'd writhed in pain on the front porch, on the verge of vomiting, and struggling to breathe. Incapacitated. Helpless. Two conditions he'd decided long ago he'd rather die than ever experience again.

But she'd done it. Gotten herself and her mother out of the house right as the fire trucks had arrived. At least he'd managed to force himself upright, albeit hunched over, to help her the last few feet so he didn't come off like a total loser.

"I'm sorry," she said, her voice gravelly from smoke inhalation, her words muffled by the oxygen mask.

Not as sorry as she was going to be. Because

once he got her alone he was going to spank her bare backside until it was a bright cherry-red for doing what she'd done.

He shifted his stance, the ache in his balls accompanied by a deep pressure low in his gut. Terrific.

"I told you this would happen, young lady," an older man wearing a red windbreaker with the words "Fire Marshal" in black across the chest said. "But did you listen? No. You thought you knew better than I did and look what happened. Your mother could have been badly burned or killed, and it would have been all your fault."

Fig waited for Roxie to put the condescending windbag in his place. But she sat in the back of the ambulance, her feet dangling, looking utterly devastated.

"Hold on there." Fig jumped to her defense. "If, in your professional opinion, this house was a fire hazard and Roxie and her mom were in imminent danger, then it was your duty to enforce whatever fire codes you have in this town and evacuate the premises. Any less speaks of negligence on your part which makes this situation your fault, not Roxie's."

"I recommended she leave," the old man said, losing some of his initial bluster.

"You gave me two weeks to clean it up," Roxie spoke.

Clean up what? Fig wondered.

"More than half that time has elapsed and it looks as if you haven't done a blessed thing."

She lowered her head.

"This isn't helping," Fig pointed out. "Do you know what started the fire?"

"We can't be sure until our investigation is complete. And all the junk inside the house is hindering our efforts." He turned to Roxie. "I don't know how you could live in those deplorable conditions."

Deplorable conditions? Fig wondered. Roxie looked over his shoulder, her expression one of mortification. "*Ay Dios mio!* Do they have to do that?"

Fig turned to see firemen dragging piles of stuff and bulging garbage bags out of the house, dumping them on the front lawn.

"We can't take a chance any smoldering ash will reignite," the fire marshal said. "And my men need room to move around in there."

Roxie closed her eyes. "I want to go to the hospital to see *Mami*."

"You're going to the hospital to get yourself checked out," Fig insisted, tired of arguing with her.

"I don't need…" More coughing.

"She's ready to go," Fig called to the paramedic. The fire marshal handed Roxie a paper. "I warned you if I didn't see a noticeable improvement I'd take action. As of this minute you are officially ordered to vacate the premises."

"Great timing," Fig said to the old man. "I bet you'd recommend she up her fire insurance coverage right about now, too, huh?"

He turned in a huff and left.

"What about my things?" Roxie called after him. "And *Mami*'s things?"

"We'll worry about that in the morning," Fig said. "I'll meet you at the hospital."

Fig glanced at the passenger seat, where a subdued Roxie reclined. He had so many questions about the condition of her house, the bags and piles of what looked like trash that firefighter after firefighter had carried into her front yard. Whose were they, and why were they inside the house? It was beyond belief, the polar opposite of his neat, orderly, obsessively clean existence.

He pushed the sight out of his mind. It didn't matter. Regardless of her situation at home, tonight she was a friend in need of a place to stay.

"You can drop me at a motel," she said sullenly, facing away from him.

"I didn't convince you to leave your mom in the capable hands of the CCU staff so I could drop you at a motel. You're coming home with me."

"*Now* you'll bring me to your place?"

He smiled, relieved she sounded a bit more like the spunky woman he was growing to like a little more each minute he spent with her. Until she added, "Right. I get it. You wanted me sober. Well, tough luck. I'm not in the mood."

"So the only reason I would bring you home with me is for sex? I couldn't possibly have the least bit of compassion for a woman left homeless by fire, for a friend who's worried about her mother? I couldn't possibly be a decent enough guy to think maybe after the night you've had you wouldn't want to be left alone in an impersonal motel room? Thanks for the compliment."

"I don't even have a change of clothes," she muttered in reply.

"I can put up with you walking around naked. I'll even join in if it makes you feel more comfortable." He watched for her response.

She turned to face him and graced him with her first smile since their argument in his car. "Opportunist."

He smiled back. "If I have to, I'm sure I can rustle you up a clean T-shirt and boxer shorts."

"Thanks," she said.

"For you? Anytime."

"Only for me?" she asked, her voice teasing. "'Cause you kind of come off like a rescues-damsels-in-distress kind of guy."

Not really, more because he didn't get out all that much than he minded doing it. "We're here." Fig pulled into the parking lot and parked in Kyle's spot.

Up in the condo, Roxie collapsed on the old sofa. "I stink like smoke. But I'm too tired to shower."

It was fast approaching five in the morning. Fig was exhausted, too. "I'll help you." Fig held out his hand. "Come."

"If only it were that easy," Roxie quipped.

"Woman, you have sex on the brain."

"It's an affliction." She placed her hand in his, and he pulled her up. "Brought on by drunkenness."

"But you're not drunk now," Fig pointed out, moving to stand in front of her, as close as he could without touching her. The room heated. Or maybe it was just him.

"No." She swallowed, but maintained eye contact. "I most definitely am not drunk now."

Fig eased his fingertips up the side of her neck, slowly, stopping to cup the area just below her ear. "So what do you think is causing it?"

She leaned into his touch and closed her eyes. "This wanting a guy—without an alcohol inducement—is new territory for me," she admitted.

Good. Fig liked to explore new territory. "Come," he said quietly. "I'll get you set up for your shower."

She covered his hand with hers. "Will you join me?" she asked.

God help him, he wanted to. But, "Not tonight." She'd been through too much, may not be thinking clearly.

"But I…"

He covered her lips with his index finger. "Shhh.

I'm trying to do the right thing here." He could remember only one other time when doing the right thing was this difficult.

Based on the appearance of her home, when Roxie exited the bathroom, Fig expected to find it trashed. Instead what he found surprised him. If he wasn't mistaken, she'd left it cleaner than when she'd entered. There was not one hair in the tub, sink or on the floor. And with her head full of thick curls it defied logic to chalk it up to pure coincidence. The mirror and counter and even the tub looked like she'd toweled them dry.

Why did she pay such close attention to the cleanliness of his home and so little to her own?

As the tepid water sluiced down his body, Fig half hoped Roxie was only pretending to be asleep when he'd checked on her and that she'd join him. He'd done the right thing in turning her away. But if she persisted—and he'd left the door unlocked, hoping she would—he'd take what she offered— he was, after all, only human—and give her triple the pleasure in return. Because he wanted to lose himself in her as much as she wanted to lose herself in him.

To his overwhelming disappointment, he began and ended his shower alone.

After toweling off Fig peeked into Kyle's bedroom again to find Roxie still asleep, her beautiful face peaceful, her lovely body resting uncovered on top of the comforter. The pull to join her on the bed, to cuddle in behind her and hold her through the night, was strong. He fought it, and in an act of willpower akin to walking away from a genie offering three life-changing wishes, Fig headed for the couch.

The somewhat stinky couch with a rogue spring that made sleep impossible, as it turned out. Which was why he was awake when Roxie padded to the kitchen, quietly took a glass from the cabinet and filled it with tap water.

"You okay?" he asked, sitting up to look at her over the back of the couch. She had an exotic beauty her wild hair and men's underclothes couldn't diminish.

"Sorry," Roxie said. "I tried not to wake you. Bad dream."

"You want to talk about it?"

"Not really. I'd rather forget about it." She pulled out a chair and sat at the table.

Fig joined her.

"I never thanked you for taking down my video." She took a sip of water.

He'd done a lot more than that. "Who told you?"

"Victoria." She smiled. "Boy, did you tick her off."

Because, while he'd deleted "Roxie Loves Coxie" from four pornographic websites, he'd left the links and attached something that would make people in this town think twice before they tried to exploit one of their own again.

"I have to say I'm touched. No one has ever spread a malicious virus on my behalf before. Malicious gossip, yes. But a computer virus? Never. Did you see the line at Frankie's Computer Fix yesterday?" She smiled again. He loved her smile, sometimes teasing, sometimes flirty, sometimes happy and fun. All the time exquisitely beautiful in the way it lit up her face.

Inconvenience them. Teach them a lesson. It's what he'd intended. "Failing to consider that employees at the hospital might try to access your video while on duty was an oversight."

"That locked up computers in the lab, Radiology and Engineering." She laughed.

On which he'd spent hours of his day yesterday working with the hospital's IT department to correct.

"I especially liked the hot-pink-and-black flashing 'Pervert' that filled the screens of the affected computers. Nice touch."

Fig crossed his arm over his midsection and bowed. "I aim to please."

Roxie stilled.

They sat in a charged silence, staring at each other until Fig asked, "You hungry?" just to get the conversation started again.

Roxie placed her elbows on the table and said, "Depends on what you're offering." She slapped her hand over her mouth. "What is wrong with me?"

"Simple human attraction. You want me," he added with a big, satisfied smile. And he wanted her right back, the proof—presently tenting his boxer shorts—impossible to hide.

"So," Roxie said, not denying it as she stood. "What do you think I should do about this attraction?"

Lick me... Ride me. "Whatever you'd like." Fig

aimed for aloof. But leaned back in his chair and opened his legs, inviting her in.

She RSVP'd in the affirmative by kneeling at his feet, reaching between his thighs and cupping him. "How are the boys?"

Fine. "In need of a little attention."

"Can I tell you how sorry I am…"

"I'd rather you show me."

She met his eyes then lowered her head. And kissed him—right where he most wanted to be kissed. "My, my," she said, setting him free. "You are not at all a figlet, are you?"

No, he wasn't. "And you owe me…" he prompted her.

She looked up at him, her eyes twinkling with laughter. "A *huge,* and I mean *huge,* apology."

Without further hesitation—thank you, thank you, thank you—she slid her mouth onto him and took him deep.

"Apology accepted," he choked out, barely capable of speech at the feel of every millimeter of his aroused flesh tightly encased in Roxie's luxurious silkiness. She released him. Then swallowed him down again, and again and again in rapid succession.

"My God." She wasn't kidding when she'd touted her skill. Or maybe he'd gone too long without, avoiding the challenges of having a woman in his life, even short-term. Either way, another couple of moves like that one and he'd be finished for the night. He plowed his fingers into her hair, gently guiding her, slowing her, taking back control.

Roxie did not relinquish it easily. "That's it," he said, lifting her head, holding her firm when she tried to go back for more. "It's my turn." And to do it the way he wanted to, Fig needed her in his bed. Naked. "Come on." He leaned forward, scooped her up and carried her toward the bedroom.

"Big *and* strong," Roxie said, wrapping her arms around his neck. "Maybe my luck is finally changing."

"Baby," Fig said, then kissed her neck. "In about half an hour you're going to feel like the luckiest woman in the world."

Roxie hoped he meant it. Fig certainly had length and girth in his favor. Whether he knew how to use them remained to be seen. He placed her on the bed. Calm. Unhurried. Time to pick up the pace.

Roxie grabbed the hem of his navy tee, planning to whip it over his head.

He stopped her. "I'd rather you didn't."

"I want to see you," she said. "Feel your skin next to mine."

"When it's dark."

The early-morning sun was already peeking through the curtains. "Then I won't be able to see you, will I?" Roxie asked.

"Exactly." He smiled and eased his weight on top of her, moved his mouth to her ear and said, "You smell so good."

"Why?" she asked in reference to why he wouldn't allow her to remove his shirt.

"It must be your natural scent. Because I used the same soap as you, and I don't smell near as scrumptious."

"I meant…"

"I know what you meant." He shimmied down her body. "You have the most amazing breasts." He cupped one and, while fondling its nipple, sucked on the tip of her other breast through her T-shirt. At the sheer pleasure of it, Roxie decided to let her request to see his chest drop. For now. When he lifted her shirt over her head, she didn't argue.

When he slid the boxer shorts he'd loaned her down her legs, she welcomed the cool air on her heated skin, welcomed his slow, confident touch.

"You're bare, too," he said in awe and brushed his fingers across her mons.

Too? The image she conjured excited her. Would he let her see? In her momentary distraction, Roxie wasn't aware Fig had opened her thighs and maneuvered himself between them. Until he kissed her. There. And rubbed his soft lips along hers.

"Lift your legs," he instructed.

She did, opening for him, eagerly awaiting his next touch.

"Like this." He closed them and turned her on her side. How did he plan to…?

Whack.

His hand connected with her backside. Hard.

"What the heck…?" She certainly hadn't expected that.

Whack.

He spanked her again.

Why was he holding her down? Did he think she wouldn't like it? Was he planning to do more than a little spanking? She tried to wiggle free, wanted to discuss boundaries.

Whack.

It felt so good.

"Don't you ever knee me in the groin again," he said.

What? He was disciplining her for real? She almost laughed.

Whack.

"And if I do?" she challenged. Hoping for more.

Whack.

Yessssssss!

"I'll do a lot worse than a few smacks on the behind." An excited tingle spread from her invigorated right butt cheek to her core. She trembled.

He noticed. "Damn it, Roxie." He removed the hand holding her down. "You're enjoying this, aren't you?"

She smiled but didn't let him see. "Please, sir. May I have another?"

"Well, that takes all the fun out of trying to teach you a lesson," he said.

"Maybe for you."

"Time for plan B," he said, spreading her thighs and settling himself between them once again.

"What might plan B entail?" Roxie asked, hoping she'd enjoy it as much as plan A, liking Fig's attempt to control her in the bedroom. *Attempt* being the operative word. Since the age of sixteen, no male had ever mastered Roxie. And no man would.

"I'm going to make you beg," Fig said.

Not likely.

"I'm going to drive you so wild with lust you'll do anything, promise me anything to let you come."

"*Let* me?" He had to be kidding.

He licked up the seam of her sex until he reached it, the epicenter of her sexual being. And he set to work. Like he'd read her instruction manual from cover to cover, he did everything right, ultimately robbing her of her capacity for speech. And since she'd started enjoying sex, Roxie couldn't remember that ever happening before. All she had to do was think it—harder—to the right—faster—deeper—don't stop—and he obeyed. They were of one mind. In sync. Absolute perfection. Her breathing heavy, she rocked beneath the onslaught. So close. Almost there. Ready, oh, so ready to explode. To release every bit of frustration with her mother, guilt over the fire and fear for the future.

Then the connection broke.

"Don't stop," she commanded, gripping his head in her hands, trying to steer him. "Higher." She could feel it building. Could taste it and smell it. "Please."

"I told you I'd make you beg."

Damn him.

He flicked his tongue in rapid little strokes. Side to side. Oh, yes! He exhaled, his breath heating her. The sensation grew again. This was it. Roxie braced herself. Ready. Finally.

He stopped.

"Say it," he said.

As if she had any clue what the heck he was talking about. "More licking. Less talking." She wanted action, not dissertation.

"I won't ever kick, knee, squeeze or touch, with intent to do harm, Fig's boys, as you call them," he said, holding perfectly still about six inches away from where he should be using his lips and tongue for far more important things than talking.

Roxie couldn't wait. Needed more. Now. She reached down between her legs to take care of herself.

"I don't think so," Fig said. Balancing on one

elbow, he took both her wrists in one hand and stopped her.

"Your danglers are safe. Okay?" Roxie panted. "From this moment forward, the only reason I will ever touch them is to worship them and slather them with my affection. Now back to work."

He chuckled.

"Pleeaassee." Roxie did, in fact, beg.

Fig did not make her wait. Good man. Super-terrific-talented man. And just so he could enjoy himself, too, Roxie wrapped her legs around his head. Just like he'd wanted.

"You are an oral sex phenomenon," Roxie said, lying on her back, her body limp, still tingling from the aftereffects of the fiercest orgasms—yes, as in plural—of recent memory. Maybe ever.

"We're not done," Fig, who lay beside her, caressing her and, although she didn't think it possible so soon, arousing her all over again, whispered seductively. "I am nowhere near done with you." His tongue traced the inner rim of her ear.

"What's your fancy?" Roxie asked. "Top. Bottom. Standing. Sitting. Dressed. Undressed."

Fig rolled on top of her, his arousal hard and

heavy. He lifted his shirt and pressed his naked chest to hers. Smooth and muscled. So good.

"Me likey." Roxie massaged the bare skin of his back while holding him close. "Kiss me," she said, wanting to taste him, to experience his luscious mouth in a new way.

He kissed her ear and the enchanting cove beneath it. He moved on to her neck and chin. He hesitated.

"Kiss me." She lifted her head to meet him halfway…and her lips connected with his cheek. Why?

Fig didn't give her time to ponder. He slid his hand between her legs and plunged his fingers inside of her. Shallow at first. Then deeper. Over and over. Each time the heel of his hand rubbed and teased and increased her stimulation exponentially. An accomplished multitasker, he used his mouth to lavish attention on her breasts.

Roxie's mind went blank. Again. Her only thought. More. "I need more," she said, rocking her hips, meeting each of his thrusts. "You." She thrust one last glorious time. "Inside." She pulled him on top of her. "Me." She tugged at his boxers. He lifted. She yanked them down.

His bare flesh met hers.

She let out a breath. "You feel so good."

"So do you." He went up on his arms, looked down at her, and rubbed her sex with the length of his, in long, lazy strokes. All too soon he rolled off of her.

"No." She made a grab for him.

"Patience, my sweet."

Aroused and wanting, the word *patience* did not exist in her vocabulary at the moment.

He reached for a condom from a drawer beside the bed and held it out to Roxie. "Care to do the honors?"

Heck yeah. She took it. "You mean they make them this big?" she asked. Because, hello, Fig had a package every man of her intimate acquaintance would envy and any woman who swung toward heterosexual would kill to have inside her. Roxie opened the wrapper and tossed it to the floor.

He smiled. "I have to special-order them."

He sounded serious, but mischief danced in his eyes.

"But do you know how to wield such a fine instrument?" She rolled the condom into place, praying he did.

"Why don't you tell me?" With a jerk of his hips,

he rested at her entrance. "You ready?" He dipped inside. A sample. A tease.

So ready. Like she'd been waiting for this moment—for him—all her life. "Impress me," she challenged.

Boy, oh, boy, did he. Fig didn't rush, his style more finesse than frenzy. Thorough and thoughtful. It worked. He watched her as he slid in and out of her body. Intense. Controlled. Like her satisfaction mattered. Like she mattered.

And, well what d'ya know? Roxie—a "sprint to the finish so we can do it again" kind of gal—relished each slow, sensual stroke. He kept her on the sublime edge, an optimum place to languish.

Then she saw it. A hitch in his facade. He thrust deep and closed his eyes. Stiffened, but not in orgasm. More like trying to regain charge of himself. Sweet man.

"Don't hold back," Roxie said, clamping her legs around his butt, locking him to her and setting a pounding pace. "I'm there. I'm ready."

Fig let out a breath, collapsed on top of her and buried his head in the side of her neck.

"Let yourself go," she said, in between panting breaths.

"My God," he said, reverence in his tone. "You are amazing."

Roxie liked the sound of that.

"I don't want to hurt you," he said.

"You can't." At least not as a result of sex. But she was growing to like him. A little too much. And with that came the probability he'd hurt her at some point. If she gave him a chance. But she wouldn't think of that now. Not while he filled her so completely and held her like he never wanted to let her go.

"I can't stop," Fig said. "I'm going to…"

"Me, too," Roxie answered. And she did. Again. But this time, it was so much better, the experience so much more powerful, because Fig accompanied her, his heated breath coming in spurts and moans against her neck, his body rigid and twitching, a comforting weight on top of her.

She felt a connection that transcended sex.

He didn't roll off of her when he was done. He didn't say something crass like, "You are one hell of a lay, Ronnie." "That's Roxie." "Sorry, honey." He didn't head for the bathroom and return carrying her clothes. He didn't offer to call her a cab or stretch and tell her how early he had to get up in the morning.

He simply lay there, nestled within her, twirling his fingers in her hair.

After a while he said, "I don't want to move. Ever."

Neither did Roxie. "No reason to." She cuddled him close. Perfectly content.

"I must be crushing you."

"I'm made of sturdy stuff." At least on the outside. Inside? Not so much.

Roxie's cell phone rang from the kitchen. She didn't want to answer, didn't want to deal with Johnny or the hospital. But it could be *Mami*. Was it too much to ask for a few minutes to enjoy some postcoital bliss? For a few peaceful, undisturbed minutes where the outside world, her problems and responsibilities didn't intrude? "I, uh, need…"

Fig lifted off of her and rolled to the side. "Go."

Roxie ran to the kitchen. "Hello," she said into the phone without looking at the display.

"Where are you?" Victoria asked, sounding frantic. "Why didn't you call me?"

"Everything happened so fast. Then it was too late."

"I am always there for you," Victoria said quietly. "No matter the time. We're friends."

Maybe Roxie didn't want her "friend" witnessing yet another of her screwups. "Fig was with me."

Victoria said nothing.

"How did you find out?" Roxie asked.

"Haven't you seen the newspaper?"

"¡Coño!" Roxie closed her eyes and leaned against the wall. Now everyone would know. "It happened at midnight. How did it make the paper?"

"I don't know but there are pictures." She paused as if considering what to say next. She settled on, "And an interview with the fire marshal. Roxie, I had no idea. What can I do to help?"

"There's nothing you can do. Nothing anyone can do. I've got to go."

"Wait," Victoria said. "I visited your mom. It occurred to me in all the years I've known you, I've never met her."

Because *Mami* didn't like strangers and rarely left the house except to go to the doctor or church. "How is she?" Roxie asked, feeling guilty that while she was enjoying herself with Fig, her mother was lying alone in a hospital bed.

"She's stable. No reports of chest pain through

the night. But she's hypertensive and anxious. She's asking for you."

"I'll get there as soon as I can."

"She wants you to bring her glasses," Victoria said. "She said you keep a spare pair in your room."

Because *Mami* kept misplacing her pair in the mess. "I will." Roxie hesitated. "Thanks." And she disconnected the call.

"Everything okay?" Fig asked, handing her a navy bathrobe.

"*Mami*'s asking for me. I've got to go. Would you drop me at my house so I can pick up my car?" And sneak in to get some clothes and *Mami*'s glasses.

Fig offered her another tee and a pair of sweatpants. They left five minutes later.

What Roxie saw when Fig pulled up to park across the street from her house was reminiscent of the newsfeed from coverage of a natural disaster. Debris littered her yard to the point there was barely any visible grass. Bags and boxes and piles of *Mami*'s "treasures" in all their broken, stained, waterlogged splendor tossed out for all to see. And there were plenty of lookers, their faces a mix of awe and revulsion.

Roxie hung her head. She should have done more, pushed harder, been more assertive in getting *Mami* to accept therapy—even though she'd made it clear she did not want or need it. Roxie should have snuck out to a Dumpster under cover of darkness and gotten rid of the bags as fast as *Mami* took them in. But even though it didn't look like *Mami* could possibly know what she had and where, she did. And when she wanted something in particular, she went looking for it. Heaven help Roxie if she didn't find it.

No one but a daughter forced to assume the caregiver role of her mentally ill mother could possibly understand the delicate balance necessary to keep the peace or how truly difficult it was to assert any type of authority over the woman who raised you. Over the years, during many a heated argument, *Mami* had threatened to kick Roxie out of "her" house.

Then who would have taken care of her? So Roxie'd resigned herself to doing the little *Mami* allowed her. It wasn't near enough.

Fig put his hand on her thigh. "I'll come in with you."

"No. I don't need you to come with me," Roxie

said, taking a deep breath and bolstering up her courage. She opened the car door and climbed out.

Fig did the same. "I want to."

"You one of those gawkers who can't stay away from a catastrophe?"

He ignored her and simply walked around the car to stand next to her. "There's the fire marshal," he pointed out.

"Oh goodie. One of my favorite people." *Favorite* as in top-five people she'd love to go a few rounds with in a no-holds-barred matchup.

"I'm going to talk to him." Fig took her hand and led her across the street.

At the edge of the driveway Roxie removed her hand from his. "I'll wait here." As soon as Fig had the fire marshal distracted, she slipped into the house, not wanting him to see the magnitude of her mother's hoarding or to know the extent of Roxie's failure to get control of the situation, failure as a daughter responsible for the care of her mother.

Despite the open windows, the pungent smell of smoke and char lingered. All the clutter from the entryway, kitchen and hallway was gone. Just like that. Simply and easily removed. While she'd spent years unsuccessfully trying to coax *Mami* to allow her to do it.

It felt odd to see the expanse of linoleum, had been years since she could walk through her house unencumbered. Roxie refused to look at the kitchen, the focal point of the blaze. She didn't want to know the extent of the damage. Not yet. Instead she walked down the hallway without having to turn to the side to squeeze past the two dollhouses and piles of towels and children's books that'd been stacked hip high prior to the fire. *Mami's* room looked the same. Untouched. Horrific. Shameful.

"It's hard to believe she actually lives in there," Fig said, standing close, looking over her shoulder.

"I asked you not to come with me. Do I need to call Victoria to have *her* ask you in order for you to listen?"

"By my recollection, you didn't ask, you ordered. I don't respond well to being told what to do," Fig said. "Where do *you* sleep?"

Since she needed to get *Mami's* glasses and change her clothes anyway, Roxie slid past him, took the key from her pocket and unlocked her door.

"You have a dead bolt on your bedroom door?" he asked. Incredulous.

The lock was the only reason her room remained immaculate, exactly the way she'd left it.

"I'm trying to understand," Fig said, his words tight, "how you can let a house get this overrun with…stuff without making any attempt to clean it."

Without making an attempt to clean it? Roxie went rigid. She cleaned it every single day. The bathroom and the kitchen, the pathways and hallway. She argued with *Mami,* every single day, to get her to part with her things, to let Roxie sort through the piles and throw away what wasn't worth saving. But *Mami* would cry and yell and clutch her heart. No one could possibly understand how hard she'd tried, day after day, year after year, to clean this house that had become the absolute bane of her existence.

"And how a daughter can allow her mother to live in such filth while she lives in this beautiful room," he added.

"*Allow?* You think I *allow* my mother to live in filth? That I have any control over what she does and how she lives?"

"The fire marshal said he's seen this before. He knows of a therapist." He held a business card out to Roxie. "Maybe she can help."

"*Me?* You think *I* need therapy? My God." This was not to be believed. "You think this mess is *my* doing? You think *I'm* the hoarder? That I'm the reason we live like this? Get out," she screamed. "Get the hell out of my house."

CHAPTER FIVE

THE fire marshal had painted a grim picture of Roxie, using words like *neglect, abuse* and *Adult Protective Services.* Fig refused to believe the jaded man's claims. Roxie was too kind and caring. But people never suspected his mother was capable of what she'd done, either. So for a few seconds, when Fig experienced the sharp contrast of Roxie's beautiful room in relation to the rest of the house, Fig allowed doubt to creep in, considered the possibility maybe he'd misjudged her. Unchecked, an accompanying rage at a person in power mistreating someone dependent upon them overtook his good sense and he'd lashed out.

But the look in her eyes confirmed what he should have known.

He'd made a terrible mistake.

Beyond her anger he saw hurt and disappointment, a deep sadness, and if Fig wasn't mistaken, there was a bit of hysteria there, too. Good thing they weren't standing in the kitchen, where death by—insert sharp object here—would have been a distinct possibility. "Calm down," he said, using his most placating tone. "I didn't mean…"

"You want calm?" Roxie yelled, slamming open her closet door to expose two rows of neatly hung clothing on equally spaced hangers. Pants with the pants. Shirts with the shirts. All sorted by color. "Well, you're not going to find it here," she continued. "You won't find anything here because this house is an abso-frigging-lute disaster area." She yanked a pair of pants off of a hanger. "And of course this mess is all *my* fault because *I'm* a hoarder. The fire marshal thinks it. You think it. After the article in the newspaper—which I have yet to see for myself—I bet the entire town thinks it." She bent down to pick up a pair of bright orange flip-flops from the neat rows of shoes on the closet floor. Sneakers with sneakers. Sandals with sandals. And so on.

"I didn't say…"

"You want calm?" she screamed again. "Then stay away from me because I am chock-full of crazy." She pulled on a drawer so hard it flew out of the dresser. She dumped its contents on the bed, sorted through what turned out to be dozens of pairs of skimpy panties and plucked out a zebra-striped thong.

Then, right there in front of him, she pushed down the sweatpants and boxers he'd loaned her, stepped out and handed them to him.

"I'm a loon. A hoarder. I live like this because I like it. I neglect and abuse my mother. Because that's just the type of low-life, uncaring daughter I am." She untangled her thong then jammed one foot followed by the other into the leg openings. "Oh," she added. "Let us not forget—" she yanked up the panties "—I'm a porn star. And a drug dealer. Come on, Fig. What else? What other terrible things can we come up with?"

Her upset seared the outer walls of his heart. But at the same time he knew Roxie needed this release, this chance to purge the bad. She'd feel better when it was over. How he'd fare remained to be seen.

She pulled on her pants. "Slut. Alcoholic." Tears streamed down her cheeks. "Illegitimate—because my *papi* denies I'm his. And why the hell are you still here?" she yelled. "Oh." She whipped the T-shirt she'd borrowed over her head and threw it at him. "You have your clothes. Now go."

She had beautiful, smooth, tan skin and pert, rounded breasts. The inner curve of the left one bore his love bite. He smiled at the memory of putting it there.

"What's so funny? You enjoying the show?" She hauled out another drawer and dumped its contents on the bed. Bras this time. In an impressive array of colors and patterns. She sorted through until she found the one that matched the panties and slipped it on.

"I hate this house." She snapped an orange-and-white-striped shirt off of a hanger. "I hate this town." She pulled it over her head. "And I hate you." She glared at him.

"I'm sorry…" Fig tried.

"Agreed." She moved to the mirror and ran a pick through her hair. "Now take your sorry self someplace else."

"Roxie, I shouldn't have…" he added.

"I shouldn't have, either." She ran an eyeliner pencil under each eye and applied some clear lip gloss. "But I've learned my lesson." She grabbed a pair of eyeglasses and a set of keys from the top of her dresser and stepped toward the door.

Fig stopped her. "Wait." She stood defiant, looking away from him. "I didn't say you were a hoarder," he said calmly. "I don't believe you're a slut or an alcoholic or an abusive/neglectful daughter. And I know you're not a drug dealer or a porn star."

He noted the tiniest hint of softening in her posture.

"I didn't say you need therapy, but from the condition of this house, someone does. I was only trying to help."

"The last thing I need is some judgmental, do-gooder pity. I don't need or want your help. And I don't need or want you." She pulled away and darted for the door. "Goodbye, Fig."

"Roxie. Wait," Fig called out and went after her.

She halted.

Not because he'd called her.

She stood completely still, staring into the charred remains of her kitchen. The entire room would need to be gutted and rebuilt.

Fig walked up beside her.

"I wish this house and everything in it had burned to the ground last night," she said quietly.

"Maybe, while your mom's in the hospital, we can bring in Dumpsters and get rid of everything," Fig suggested.

She glared at him. "If it was as easy as bringing in Dumpsters and throwing everything out, don't you think I'd have done that by now? You really don't think much of me, do you?" She turned toward the door.

Fig reached for her arm. Again. "Please," he said. "Help me to understand. When did it start? How did it get this bad?"

Roxie let out a breath and looked down at the floor. "Apparently it started after *Mami*'s husband—my alleged *papi*—left her, before I was born. She refused to get rid of his stuff and continued to buy him clothes and presents, anticipating his return. Growing up, it was like he still lived here. His slippers rested on the floor in front of his recliner—" she pointed into the mounds of junk in the far corner of what may have been a family room at one time "—which is over there somewhere." She laughed. "For all I know they're probably still there." She paused. "His favorite coffee mug—from the manufacturer of his favorite bowling ball—sat next to the coffeepot. His winter coat hung in the closet. Come to think of it, that's probably still there, too."

"She was trying to hold on to her life before he'd left," Fig surmised.

"She paid more attention to the past than she did to the present. Which is why my brothers got out of here first chance they got."

"Leaving you behind."

She nodded. "Then *Mami* started doing the same for each of them. Buying things—with money she didn't have—in an attempt to entice them home to visit."

Which was why Roxie wound up sleeping with a grocer for food. Fig's initial reaction was the woman needed some sense pounded into her. But he knew, from experience, the complex challenge of dealing with a mentally ill mother.

"When she'd spent down all her savings and the money she'd gotten from refinancing the mortgage on the house, she started asking for donations of clothing, housewares and children's toys from the church."

"How old were you when your brothers left home?"

"The youngest one moved out when I was ten.

That's when stuff really started to pile up. I tried—" she sniffed "—to stop her. To throw things out. But I was a kid and she can get mean and aggressive."

Fig put his arm around her shoulders and directed her back to her bedroom, the only place clean enough for them to sit down. "Tell me why the fire marshal thinks *you're* the hoarder."

Roxie shrugged. "When he came to the house after the first fire…"

"The first fire?"

Roxie nodded. "*Mami*'s been getting more forgetful. A week ago she burned her lunch, which is why I removed the knobs from the stove. It was more smoke than anything." She waved it off. "Anyway, *Mami* refused to speak to him. She wouldn't leave her room. She just sat there, looking down at her feet, fidgeting, rocking." She looked up at him. "She does that when she gets stressed. *Mami* doesn't like strangers in her home."

They entered Roxie's room.

"*Mami* started rubbing her chest in the way she does when her angina is coming on. I did what I had to do to get the men to leave. I took responsibility and said I'd clean out the house."

Roxie sat on her bed, lifted one of her drawers

onto her lap and started to fill it with her bras. "He gave me two weeks."

Two weeks? It'd take at least a dozen people working day and night to clean out the house in two weeks. No wonder she'd been preoccupied at work. Fig sat next to her, lifted the other drawer onto his lap and said, "Let me help you."

Roxie smirked. "Can't pass up an opportunity to paw at my panties, can you?"

Fig smiled. "Guilty." He got to work. "Why do you stay?" he asked, knowing the answer.

Roxie shrugged. "She's my mom. She has her problems, but deep down I know she loves me. And I love her."

He understood completely.

"When I graduated high school I thought about leaving, like my brothers had. But then who would have shopped and cooked and cleaned up around here? I know it doesn't look like I do anything, but I keep the kitchen counter clear so I have room to prepare our meals. I keep the refrigerator clean and do the dishes. I maintain the paths so *Mami* doesn't trip and fall and I keep the clutter out of the bathroom. It takes a lot more time and effort than you'd think."

"I'm sure it does."

She looked at him askance. "She doesn't work. Hasn't worked since I got my first job at sixteen. Her health is deteriorating. What would happen to her if I left?"

She'd become a ward of the state, and they'd have to deal with her. But Roxie was too good a daughter to let that happen. "She's lucky to have you."

"Yeah. Yeah." Roxie downplayed her worth, stood and replaced her drawer in her dresser. Fig replaced the one beside it.

"So what happens now?" Fig asked.

Roxie held up a pair of glasses. "Now I go to the hospital to check on *Mami* and give her her glasses."

"I mean what are you going to do about the house and the mess outside? Oh, and I forgot to mention, the fire marshal said upon inspection this morning, the house is structurally sound. You can't return to live here, but you can come and go between the hours of nine and five as long as you don't use any electricity."

At least that was something.

"Where will you stay?" Fig asked. "Where will

your mom stay when she's released from the hospital?"

"I'll work it out." She stood. Everything always worked out. Somehow. "No need to worry about me."

"You're welcome to stay at my place. I'll take the couch." But he'd rather not.

"What fun would that be?"

Thank you! "Or I could make myself available for stress relief after a long, hard day."

"Or at the start of one." She smiled back.

"Anytime," Fig clarified and meant it.

"What about right now? What if I were to say 'I want you now. Hard and fast and I'm in charge.' What then?"

Fig stood up, walked to the door, closed and locked it. It'd be unrealistic to expect to control a woman with Roxie's passion every time. Part of focusing on the woman involved knowing when she needed to take the lead.

"Just like that?" Roxie asked. "I say I want sex, you drop your pants and we go at it?"

If that's what she needed. "I know how you feel, Roxie."

She laughed. "How could you possibly know how I'm feeling?"

"Because I've been there."

"Where exactly is *there?*"

"Living with a mother who cared more about herself and her needs than she did mine. Living the life she'd created for me rather than my own life. Feeling let down and angry and betrayed by my family. Feeling my life was going nowhere but too tired to fight for what I wanted."

After a few moments of silence, she said, "Which hits home the fact you know a lot more about me than I know about you. I want three questions, and you have to answer honestly."

"I'd rather you use me for sex."

She smiled playfully. "We can make them strip questions, you know, since the door's already locked."

All he'd have to do was answer three simple questions to get her naked. "Your bra and panties count as undergarments. That's one item of clothing."

"Fine. When we first met and I asked you out to dinner, why did you say you were dying of cancer?"

"Because my medical history usually freaks people out. But you looked like you could handle it. So I made a joke to see how you'd react."

"For the record, jokes are supposed to be funny. That wasn't. You'd do better with a different approach."

"You handled it just fine."

"Well, I'm not your typical woman, am I?"

No, she wasn't. "Is that your second question?" He smiled. "Because you need to take off your shirt before I'll answer another one."

"No, that's not my second question," she grumbled as she lifted her shirt over her head to expose her well-endowed, zebra-print-bra-covered breasts.

"Is your medical history the reason you're so pale and have no hair?"

"Childhood leukemia. In and out of remission. Radiation therapy. Chemotherapy. Bone-marrow transplantation resulting in permanent remission but accompanied by permanent alopecia—but I'd like to point out, freak that I am, I somehow retained my eyebrows and eyelashes." Both of which he bleached to a pale blond or they looked odd on his pigment-challenged face. "I'm pale because I grew up the boy in the proverbial bubble. I rarely went outside except to go to the doctor or the hospital. I developed indoor interests that I continue to enjoy as an adult."

Roxie looked sad. This time for him.

"None of that, sweetheart," he said, hating pity. "Now give up your pants."

She smiled as she stood. "Pushy, pushy." She shimmied out of her cargo pants. Lord help him, she had a beautiful body. Tall and slender yet rounded in all the right spots. A body he dreamed about and would no doubt continue to dream about long after he returned home.

He reached for her.

"Nuh, uh, uh." She wagged a finger between them. "I have one more question."

"Well, spit it out. You expect too much if you think me capable of sitting politely when you are looking so good and so naked and all I have to do is extend my arm this much to touch you." He poked her on the shoulder.

She reached behind her back, undid her bra and flung it at him. "To sweeten the pot."

"This last one must be a doozy." He eyed her breasts, imagined each one filling his palm. "Go ahead. I'm ready."

"Why wouldn't you take off your shirt for me this morning?"

Fig let out a breath and tried to think of a way to get out of answering. But the determined look on Roxie's face left no doubt if he didn't answer they would not be having sex. If he wanted Roxie, and, oh, did he want Roxie, he'd have to explain. Or he could simply go ahead and show her. Roxie was different. Maybe the sight of his torso wouldn't appall her like it had the few women he'd shared it with.

He reached for the bottom hem of his tee.

Roxie could not believe her eyes and, yes, could not stop her mouth from dropping open in surprise. "You're…" The words wouldn't come.

Fig stood there, staring back at her, looking vulnerable and so uncomfortable under her perusal.

"I have scars and…I'll put my shirt back on."

Roxie ripped it from his hands and tossed it over her shoulder. "From now on," she said, stepping close enough to touch him, "when we're together, I want you shirtless." She traced some of the outlines with her finger. "*You* are a thing of beauty, a colorful canvas to be ogled and appreciated, not hidden."

Brilliantly colored, professionally crafted tattoos, interwoven with scrolls on which motivational proverbs were expertly written, covered his chest and shoulders to the point they obliterated his pallor. Yet no hint of this amazing profusion of color extended past the short sleeves or neckline of his T-shirt. Which made her wonder, "Your legs?"

He nodded. "I needed some color."

Roxie dropped her hands to the button of his pants. "I am a huge fan of color." She had his pants down to his ankles in a matter of seconds. A realistic-looking python, surrounded by various shades of brilliant-green foliage, circled his left thigh. The tail of a fire-breathing red dragon, set against a mountain of rock, circled his right. Both tattoos ended just above his knee. "Why do you hide them?"

Fig shrugged. "Tattoo art is not an acceptable form of expression among my business associates, friends and family."

"Then you need to find some new people to hang around with." He was…beautiful and so different than he appeared at first sight.

"There's one more," Fig said, sounding hesitant. "On my back."

"Let me see. Let me see." Roxie rubbed her hands in anticipation.

He took his sweet time showing her. But when he did… Roxie sucked in a breath. Absolutely magnificent.

"It's a phoenix," Fig explained.

A beautifully drawn, intricately detailed phoenix rising up from flames. Reborn. The image filled Fig's back, the mythical bird's plumage inked in vibrant reds, oranges and golds. Its wings extended, spanning his shoulders.

"You're awful quiet." He turned his head to try to look at her. "I chose a phoenix because each time the doctors had thought I wouldn't make it, I pulled through, came back from the dead in a sense."

Roxie set her palms to his skin and caressed the bird. Felt something up by its beak. Stopped.

"I was in a car accident," Fig said. "I received over a hundred and seventeen stiches."

"I'm so sorry."

"Don't be." He turned to face her. "It's how I met Kyle. In rehab." He lifted her hand to his left upper chest. Another scar. "This one's from the portacath the doctors inserted for my chemo."

Roxie kissed it.

Her phone rang.

Not now. She dropped her forehead to his chest. He kissed the top of her head. "You'd better answer that," he said.

Most men would have told her not to answer it. But Fig understood. "I know. But I don't want to." They'd each shared a part of themselves. Things she hadn't shared with another person. And Roxie got the impression Fig didn't share his tattoos with many people, either. Yet he'd shared them with her. She felt so close to him right now and didn't want it to end. But the call could be from *Mami*. Roxie picked up the phone and checked the voice mail. *Mami* asked, "Where are you? What's taking so long? I can't see the TV up close without my glasses."

"I have to go," Roxie told Fig.

"I know," Fig answered, pulling up his pants.

"Tonight?" Roxie asked. She'd make this interruption up to him then.

"Most definitely."

After helping Roxie pack a small duffel and bag

up some clothes to wash, Roxie let Fig drive her to the hospital. Yes, she could have driven herself. But then he wouldn't be holding her hand and she wouldn't be feeling so…happily content.

"If your mom wasn't in the picture," Fig said, "where would you be living? What would you be doing?"

"I stopped wishing for a different life years ago." She never understood people who wasted their time pining for a life they couldn't have. Better to accept the life you did have and make the best of it.

He squeezed her hand. "Humor me."

Okay. "Tightrope walker traveling with the circus. Roller Derby queen. Llama farmer."

"Come on, Roxie."

"All right. I'd still be a nurse because I love it. But I wouldn't live anywhere near Madrin Falls. This town holds very few happy memories for me." She looked over at him. "Although today increased the count by two."

He smiled. "I'm glad."

"I think I'd like to live someplace warm. In a condo by the beach. Where I could parade around in skimpy bathing suits and sip iced drinks beside a pool every day if I felt like it."

"I'd risk blistering sunburns to come and watch you parade around in those skimpy bathing suits."

"Well, I'd rub you from head to toe with SPF 50—" just like in her dream "—to protect your beautiful skin. And I'd invest in a huge beach umbrella." Wouldn't that be fun. The two of them. Hot days at the beach. Hotter nights. Together. Naked.

"Honey, you'd better let me apply my own sunscreen or we'll be spending more time indoors than out."

Fig veered onto the hospital drive and reality slammed back into the forefront. There was no condo, no beach and no iced drinks by the pool in Roxie's immediate future.

At the block of elevators in the lobby, Roxie pushed three for the CCU. Fig pushed five. Roxie looked up at him.

"I have an appointment," he said. "Do you want me to meet you over in CCU when I'm done? Or should I wait in the lobby?"

Who could he possibly have an appointment with on the fifth floor? Victoria? She studied him, but he gave nothing away. Was there some meeting—that she apparently was not privy to—where her future at Madrin Memorial was to be decided? And if that were the case, why hadn't Fig told her?

"It's nothing important." He pulled her close and kissed the top of her head. "I'll miss you," he whispered.

Although it was hard to fathom, she felt a pang of loss at their separation, too.

"Hola, Mami." Roxie channeled good cheer as she entered the single-bedded room, noting the wires emerging from beneath her mother's hospital gown winding up to the cardiac monitor flashing on the wall. Heart rate eighty-two. Normal sinus rhythm. Good.

"I have no privacy here," *Mami* complained, motioning to the glass half of the wall overlooking the nurses' station. "I want to go home."

"According to your nurse, the doctor wants to keep you for at least another day so you can have a few more respiratory treatments." Which gave Roxie one more day to figure out what to do with *Mami* after discharge.

"I don't want to stay." She sat up, slid her legs over the side of the bed and started to push off.

"Stop," Roxie said, rushing to the other side of the bed and holding *Mami* by the shoulders. "At the moment, our home is uninhabitable." The fire marshal had his scrawling signature on an official paper saying so.

"What does that mean?" *Mami* suddenly looked very old and weak in that big hospital bed.

"Lie back down." Roxie got her propped up on her pillows and tucked the covers around her. "It means we can't live in the house until we clean it enough that the fire marshal says it's not a safety hazard for you to live there." And until Roxie settled with the insurance company—who had deemed two fires in two weeks suspicious—so she could replace the kitchen.

"It's *my* house."

Technically it was Roxie's house since *Mami* signed it over to her when she'd turned eighteen—to keep her creditors from going after it.

"Where will we go?" *Mami* clutched her chest. Roxie detected an arrhythmic change in the blip of the cardiac monitor. "*Ay Dios mio.* What will happen to us? To all our things?"

"Calm down," Roxie said, caressing her thinning gray hair. "We are going to be fine. I'll take care of everything." Like she always did.

"It's already taken care of." Fig entered the room.

"Victoria's offered to have your mom stay at her house."

What? "That's where you went? To talk to Victoria?"

Fig nodded.

"Why didn't you tell me?"

"Because you would have told me not to."

He was right. Roxie didn't like imposing on her friends.

"Who are you?" *Mami* asked Fig.

"The name's Fig." He held out his hand. She took it. Hesitantly. "I'm a friend of Roxie's."

"You're so pale."

"Mami!"

"You need to eat some meat. I want to cook you a steak."

The woman in the bed looked like her mother, but that last comment had Roxie questioning her true identity. "You haven't cooked a steak in over ten years." Hadn't cooked much of anything besides macaroni and cheese, grilled cheese and canned soup.

"Because I haven't had a man around to cook for." So the daughter who took care of her day after day didn't rate a delicious steak dinner. Good to know.

"I'm sorry, but I don't eat meat, Mrs. Morano."

Come to think of it, she hadn't seen him eat much of anything.

"Which is why you're so pale," *Mami* said.

No, he wasn't. Not really. He was bright and colorful and she loved that he kept it secret from the world, yet shared it with her. "We were talking about Victoria."

"Is that the nice young lady who visited me this morning? A tiny thing with black hair?"

Roxie couldn't believe she remembered. "That's her."

"We can both stay there?"

"No," Fig answered. "I'm afraid she only has space for one. But you'll have your own room and television and there's a full bath just down the hall."

"I couldn't…" *Mami* started. "I want to stay with Roxie. Where will you be?" she asked.

Fig raised one of his bleached brows.

"With a friend," Roxie said, avoiding eye contact. *Mami* still preached the importance of Roxie remaining chaste for her future husband. Like any man in this town would marry her after the life she'd lived to date—and with her hoarding mother in tow. "She has a small place. Only one bedroom." At least that last part was true.

"She's very nice to take you into such cramped quarters," Fig commented with a smirk.

"More like desperate for company," Roxie said. "She's kind of an oddball. I actually feel a little sorry for her."

"You'd really be helping Victoria," Fig said, ignoring her last comment. "School's out and she could use some help keeping an eye on her son until summer camp starts, and if you're there long enough, maybe after camp."

Mami's face lit up. "How old is the boy?"

"Nine," Roxie answered. "But I don't think…" She wasn't well, mentally or physically.

"That's the same age as Angelo." One of the many grandchildren they'd seen only in Christmas card photos. "I'll do it," *Mami* said, looking happier than Roxie had seen her in years.

But still. "You're not up to babysitting." She could barely take care of herself.

"May I speak with you in private?" Fig asked.

What was he up to? Roxie followed him out into the hallway.

"Victoria wants to do this," he said, taking her hand. "She said when she visited your mother this morning she'd perked up at the mention of Jake—" Victoria's son "—and she thought if we could convince your mom she'll be helping out with Jake, it may sway her decision. Victoria assured me she will make sure both your mom and Jake are well supervised and safe."

Safe was good. "But she'd be taking Kyle's room." Since Victoria wouldn't let her fiancé sleep upstairs with her until they were officially married.

"Kyle loves the idea of giving up his room. And having you and me at his condo so Victoria has no choice but to welcome him in her bed."

"Did she agree to that?" Because it wasn't like her friend to stray from a plan.

"Not yet. But she will."

"You two are such schemers." Who had grossly underestimated Victoria's resolve.

"Kyle gets to sleep with Victoria. Your mom has a place to stay until we get the house cleaned out and fixed up. It's a win-win."

We. Roxie'd done so much on her own, for so

long, was so tired… She almost collapsed against him at the word *we*.

"Come on. We need to talk to your mom about the house."

There it was again. *We*. Although, "I think we should wait. She's not strong enough."

"She looks strong enough to me. If I'm wrong, there are plenty of doctors and nurses who will swarm the room at the first sign of trouble."

"Maybe I should talk to her in private."

"Maybe having someone else in on the conversation will help."

It was worth a try. "But if it upsets her—" like Roxie anticipated it would "—we drop it."

"Let's play it by ear." Fig led her back into the room.

"*Mami,* we need to talk about what we're going to do with all the…stuff that's accumulated in the house over the years."

She clamped her lips together and glanced nervously at Fig.

"I think you're a truly special lady for working so hard to acquire things for your boys," Fig said. "But we need to find a way to get all the clothing and toys to them so they can put it to good use."

Mami relaxed. Roxie could have kissed Fig.

"My boys need to come home. So I can show them everything I have for them."

"I'll make a deal with you, Mrs. Morano. If you work with Roxie and me and a few of our friends to sort through all the items in your house and divide them into what goes to which son, I promise to get your boys to come and pick it all up personally."

Not "I promise to try" or "I promise to do my best," but "I promise to get your boys to come." As if Roxie hadn't been trying to do just that for years. What the heck made him think he'd succeed when she couldn't? Roxie swung from wanting to kiss him to wanting to snap his neck. "May I speak with you outside?" Once there she turned on him. "What the heck were you thinking?"

"Trust me," he said.

"The words 'I promise' and 'trust me' coming out of a man's mouth don't mean a whole hell of a lot to me. But when you say 'I promise' to my mother, she'll believe you, and I won't stand by and see her hurt and disappointed when you can't deliver." Like she'd been all the times Roxie had thought her brothers would finally come through for *her* after they'd spewed their worthless "trust mes" and "I promises."

"Well, you can believe them when they come from me." Roxie started to say something but he cut her off. "I have a plan. I'm sure it will work."

CHAPTER SIX

AFTER they left the hospital, Fig made Roxie breakfast back at the condo. Then they took advantage of having her house to themselves to do some preliminary cleanup.

"I think there's a push broom in here somewhere," Roxie said, crawling across a mound of bulging plastic garbage bags into the far corner of what he'd learned was the family room.

Fig walked down the hall. "What's behind this door?" He tried the knob.

"No!" Roxie yelled. "Don't go in there."

But he'd already shouldered open a space large enough for him to stick his head inside. Unbelievable. Bags and boxes and loose…stuff were piled from floor to ceiling in every corner, chest high up to the window on the far wall, sloping down to thigh high around the door. Dust motes hung in the air, illuminated by the sunlight. Based on the dank smell and the layer of dust covering everything, that door hadn't been opened in years. He sneezed.

"Step away from that door," Roxie ordered, awkwardly trying to hurry to flat, stable ground.

"This door?" Fig pushed on it again in an attempt to create an opening big enough for him to squeeze through. When he succeeded, he slipped inside. As soon as he released his hold on it, under the weight of more bulging white garbage bags stuffed with clothes, the door promptly slammed behind him.

Roxie knocked. "Are you okay?"

"Afraid I was sucked inside by the monster behind the door?"

"Ha-ha. Open up."

"Easier said than done." He bent to lift some bags to toss them away to make room. Only, each time he moved one, something or things slid into its place. He sneezed again.

"Please tell me you're not allergic to dust," Roxie said through the door. "I told you to buy yourself a mask when we picked up the work gloves and cleaning supplies."

He hadn't wanted to insult her by wearing a mask in her home. The gloves, however—two pairs—were a necessity. A few minutes later he had enough of an area cleared to fully open the door.

Roxie walked in, her eyes wide. "Holy cow."

"How long has it been since you've been in here?"

"Seven years."

Fig climbed up on two stacks of old newspapers to survey the mess from a higher vantage point.

"Articles from Dad's bowling wins and the boys' sporting events," Roxy said.

He picked his way deeper into the room, climbed over an old red metal tricycle. Something tilted beneath him. He started to slide and caught hold of the head on a life-size plastic Santa to steady himself.

"Be careful," Roxie cautioned. "Where are you going?"

"To open the window to get some fresh air in here."

He climbed higher, slower, the piles more unstable. To the left he noticed a softball-sized hole in the corner where the ceiling met the outer wall. He pointed. "I think you may have something living in here." He scanned the room for movement, but seeing none he continued on.

"I'm going to get my broom," Roxie said. "Just in case," she called out from the hallway.

Fig came across some old *Playboy* magazines, and like any red-blooded heterosexual male, he paused to look through one.

"What's that?" Roxie asked.

He turned the magazine to the side and opened the centerfold. "Yowza!"

"What is it with men and nudie pictures? The sooner we get done, the sooner you can have the real thing. Now get crack-a-lackin'. We only have a few hours until we have to vacate the premises for the night."

With the incentive of having Roxie again, soon, Fig tossed the mag and made haste. Something on his right moved. A globe started to roll, revealing a... *"Raccoooooon!"*

Fig backpedaled to avoid its vicious fangs, turned and ran.

Roxie started up the incline, her broom overhead. "Ee-yah," she yelled like some warrior cry to battle and half ran, half climbed toward him, whacking the broom in the vicinity of the vermin. His fierce protector.

Fig leaped over the tricycle, well, at least he

tried to. Unfortunately his foot caught on something, and he came down hard on his right wrist. Damn, that hurt. He struggled to stand. Something gave way beneath him and he was going down again. This time backward, all the way to the carpet below. Oomph. On impact, all the air left his lungs. Papers and clothes and God only knew what else piled on top of him.

"Fig?" Roxie called out.

He couldn't answer.

"You'd better not be fooling around," Roxie threatened.

He moved something off his face and tried to suck in a breath.

"Holy crap," Roxie said. "I can see the headlines now. 'Man Smothered to Death in Hoarding House after Raccoon Attack.'"

With all the debris closing in around him, it felt like a distinct possibility. He tried to relax, to remain calm while he waited for his lungs to regain function.

A hand plowed through his covering and touched his face. "Nod if you're okay."

He did.

"Thank God. We've got to get you out of there.

That raccoon may have friends or babies. There may be a whole network of tunnels down there."

Shoot. He hadn't thought of that. Fig forced in a breath and elbowed some space around him so he could move. If nothing else, the commotion should keep the critters away.

He felt Roxie lifting things off of him from above.

He moved something off his belly. Pain shot from his right wrist up his arm. Not good. "Oh. Look," he said, eyeing the object. "An old-style toy car garage. I used to have one of these." He'd played with it for hours at a time, loved that toy.

"You think you could focus on getting out of there? I refuse to take responsibility for you getting bitten by anything while you're reminiscing about your childhood."

Right. The raccoon.

Fig managed to sit up and pop his head out. Ahhhh. Fresh—well, fresher than down below—air.

"Hey, there, handsome," Roxie said with a smile. She held out her hand to him.

He took it. With his right hand. Big mistake. Excruciating pain. "Ow. Ow. Ow. Let go."

"What's wrong?"

"I twisted my wrist. Nothing serious." He reached up with his other hand. She tugged and he stood.

"Let me see."

"It's nothing."

"Now."

He held out his wrist. It hung in an unnatural position.

She cupped it gently. "This doesn't look good." She ran a finger—oh, so lightly—over a lump forming on his lower forearm just before his wrist. "I'm taking you to the hospital for an X-ray."

Fig stepped back. "Oh, no, you're not. It's not broken. I am not going to the emergency room." As a patient. Ever again. A cold chill washed over him.

"Oh, yes, you are," Roxie said. Determined. "Right after I figure out where that raccoon went."

She was a persistent pain in the patoot. Fig sat at the bottom of the stretcher, his jeans and sneakers still on, but a hospital gown replaced his T-shirt. At least she'd gotten him a small private room with a window to the outside.

"So tell me again why you ran?" she asked innocently.

"Because raccoons have rabies."

Roxie held up the realistic-looking stuffed animal that'd turned out to be the cause of his current predicament. "Only the live ones," she said with a smile.

"That thing was moving," he insisted.

"Only in your imagination."

"He looked up at me."

"With glass eyes." Roxie snickered. "Probably manufactured in China." She full out laughed.

"Go ahead. Get it all out. I'm glad you find this so amusing."

Roxie struggled to catch her breath. "Raccoooooon," she imitated him, tears leaking out of her eyes.

"Get out," Fig said but without heat because he didn't really want her to leave. She kept him occupied, so he didn't spend all his time thinking about the antiseptic hospital smell. The cool, functional room. The stretcher. The coarse sheets. And the feeling of pending incarceration that accompanied them.

"I'm sorry." Roxie walked to the counter by the sink and plucked two tissues from the box.

"Really." She blotted the inner corner of each eye. "I'm sorry. It's just not every day someone I know fractures a bone trying to escape a stuffie." She turned away, her shoulders bouncing in silent laughter.

"Yes. Please. Let's focus on the outcome of this fiasco. Fractured right distal radius." He held up his damaged appendage. "In need of surgical repair. I'm right-hand dominant. I work on computers for a living." So what if he wasn't involved in any high-priority projects at the moment and he had enough money—thank you, Grandma Rose—that he didn't have to work another day in his life if he didn't want to? Having his right arm incapacitated was going to be a major inconvenience.

"Excuse me. Don't you go looking for sympathy now, Mr. It's-not-broken-I'm-not-going-to-the-emergency-room."

"See. This is why I didn't want to come. It's like taking the car to a mechanic. They always find something wrong."

"Hello. There is something wrong. You have a broken bone."

"I don't want to be here." He didn't want surgery,

didn't want Roxie to feel like she had to take care of him. He wanted to be taking care of her, helping to get her house in order.

"I know." She walked over to the stretcher and took his good hand in hers.

"So joke time is finally over?"

Roxie nodded. "But the next time I see a raccoon you can bet it'll start up all over again."

At least she wasn't looking at him with sympathy and fawning all over him.

"I can't wait."

Dr. Jared Padget, Roxie's friend and the E.R. doc on duty, entered the room. He pointed at the stuffed raccoon propped up on the over-the-bed table. "That the little guy who caused all this trouble?"

"Yeah. Wasn't it nice of Roxie to bring it to the hospital with us?" Fig asked, picking up the culprit with his left hand and lobbing it into the plastic trash container. Swish. Two points.

"Hey," Roxie said. "You're going to have to explain to *Mami* why her favorite stuffed raccoon's gone missing."

"She loves it so much she kept it locked in a room for seven years?"

"You may find it hard to believe she knows exactly what she has, but she does."

"I've got good news and bad news," Dr. Padget interjected. "Which do you want first?"

No bad news. Fig's skin started to prickle. His heart started to pound. This is how it happened. You go in for one thing and they find something else. Mass on the lung. Out-of-whack blood count. We need to admit him. The air felt too thick to reach his lungs.

"You okay?" Roxie asked, looking down at his hand with concern, which was when he realized he had such a tight grip on her, the tips of her fingers had turned a deep red.

He eased up but didn't release her. Couldn't. He swallowed. "Good news first, please."

"Dr. Rosen agreed to take you on," Dr. Padget said to Fig. "As a professional courtesy to Miz Roxie." He inclined his head in Roxie's direction. "You're scheduled for surgery at four-thirty this afternoon."

"Four-thirty?" Fig looked at his watch. "That's in three hours." What the heck was he supposed to do locked in this room for three more friggin' hours? "Please tell me I can leave and come back."

"We're not busy. It's easier if you sit tight and we'll send you up when the O.R. is ready for you."

"Easier for who?" He wanted to leave. To get in his car and drive as far as he could on whatever gas he had in the tank. Because filling up left-handed would be awkward. Damn. "Is that the bad news? That I'm stuck here?"

Dr. Padget glanced at Roxie. "Uh, no."

Great.

"Based on your mechanism of injury and your past medical history, I suspect, and Dr. Rosen concurs, that you may be suffering from some degree of osteoporosis as a long-term effect of your childhood cancer treatment."

Fig stiffened. Osteoporosis was an old-lady disease, wasn't it? Was he destined for a back hump like his grandmother? "What does that mean?"

"That you may, and we won't know for certain until we do a bone density test, have a decrease in skeletal bone mass that puts you at an increased risk for bone fractures. It would explain why a young, strong, seemingly healthy man sustained your severity of injury from a relatively minor fall."

"What does a bone density test entail?" Fig

asked. Long, thick needles, no doubt. He remembered them well. And pain. Lots of pain. Nausea threatened.

"A simple X-ray. Or more technically, a dual energy X-ray absorption or DEXA scan."

Fig exhaled.

Roxie squeezed his hand. "It doesn't have to be done today, right?" she asked.

"No," Dr. Padget said. "But soon. Depending on the test result, your primary doctor may want to start you on a combined medication and exercise regimen to slow down the bone loss and decrease your risk of additional fractures."

"I'll take care of it as soon as I get home."

When the door closed behind Dr. Padget, Roxie said, "Not a big fan of hospitals, are you?"

Fig shook his head. "I've spent way too much time in them over the years. You sure you can't slip me out for an hour or two? I need a shower. I feel all grungy." Caked with dust and scented with mildew. If nothing else, at least he could wash his hands. Fig stood and walked to the sink, reached for the handle. "Damn it." Pain stabbed through his right wrist and forearm.

"That's why Dr. P. doesn't want you out and about. Bang your wrist and you risk increasing the displacement of your fracture." Roxie shut off the water. "Let me get your nurse to give you some pain medication."

"No," he snapped. He would not take anything that would alter his cognitive function. *Roxie isn't your mother,* his rational self attempted to make him see reason. But so far Kyle was the only one who'd been able to earn Fig's trust. And that'd taken years.

"My, you're a cranky patient. Sit." She tried to guide him back to the stretcher.

He stood firm. "I'd rather stand." Tall and proud and healthy. Not wounded and weak, or dependent and vulnerable. A victim.

"Give me a few minutes. I've got to run and get some things then I'll be back to get you all settled and you can relax until surgery."

Relax. Fat chance.

In Roxie's absence, Fig paced, holding his right elbow bent and his hand elevated or it started to throb. Three steps to the window. Pivot. Three steps to the door. Pivot. Repeat. And with each forward progression he asked himself, *What am I going to do about Roxie?*

Having her sleep over when she had no place else to go and so he could take care of her was okay, but having her puttering around Kyle's condo when he wasn't up to watching her and keeping in charge of her was something else entirely.

So far the issue of her preparing food for him hadn't come up. Was it too much to hope Roxie didn't like to cook? His stomach tightened. She wouldn't understand. He'd no doubt hurt her feelings, and she didn't need him adding to her current aggravation. He liked her, but he needed to keep things casual. Friends only—preferably friends who only had sex—nothing more. He'd found that to be the easiest way to conceal his...issues. Unfortunately, most women didn't buy into the arrangement for long.

He'd lost track of how many laps he'd done—somewhere up in the hundreds—and still he hadn't come up with any stupendous ideas by the time she returned, carrying two pink plastic basins filled with soap, lotion and washcloths. Over her shoulder rested at least a dozen towels.

"What's all that for?" he asked.

"I ran up to the O.R. to get you some scrub pants. I'm going to give you a bed bath and help you get changed."

"Like hell you are," Fig said, sounding all big and tough. "I am not a child. Nor am I incapacitated. I do not need to be given a bath."

Roxie had been a nurse long enough to know when someone was scared. And she wanted to help. "Maybe not, but in addition to getting you all cleaned up, it will relax you. I promise." Roxie would make sure of it. "People say I give one primo bed bath." She walked to the lone chair in the room and unloaded her towels.

"I bet they do." His words, coated with sarcasm and heavy with sexual innuendo, hit their mark.

While she knew he was only lashing out due to his own inner struggles, his words hurt. "What's that supposed to mean?" Roxie dropped the two basins, soap and lotion onto the counter by the sink. "I'm such a tramp you think I'd behave unprofessionally while bathing a patient? That I would take advantage of someone in my care by making inappropriate, unwanted sexual advances?"

"I didn't mean…"

"Well, what did you mean, then?" Roxie glared at him, her arms crossed over her chest, and she waited for him to answer.

"I'm an ass," Fig said, sitting heavily on the stretcher, looking down at the floor. "I'm sorry."

"I get it," Roxie said. "You're tense and uncomfortable and unhappy. I feel terrible even though I didn't ask you to get involved cleaning at my house, you insisted. And I told you not to go into that room, yet you went in anyway. I am trying to do what I can to make this easier for you. But I'll be damned if I'm going to stick around and be insulted just because you're in a bad mood."

Fig toed off his sneakers. "Okay." He lay down on the stretcher, resting his right wrist on his belly. "If you think it will help, you can give me a bed bath."

You can give me. "Oh, I *can,* can I? Maybe now I don't want to. There are lots of other things I could be doing right now." But none she'd *rather* be doing.

"Do you want my pants off or on?" he asked.

"Makes no difference to me."

He reached down with his left hand and fumbled

with the button to his jeans. "You're going to stand there and watch me struggle?"

"Yes." It'd serve him right.

"No, you're not." He stared up at her. "Because you're too nice. And caring. And not at all mean. Come here," he said. Contrite. Not a command. A plea. "Please."

Her legs walked over to the stretcher.

"Don't leave me," he said quietly. "I need you."

That was all she had to hear. Roxie moved to the head of the bed, kissed his forehead and said, "You've got me." The idea excited her. Felt kind of girlfriendy. A new gig for her. She kinda liked the thought of taking care of him—her temporary man—looked forward to staying with him after surgery, to cooking and cleaning up after someone who'd actually appreciate it.

Roxie walked to the sink, adjusted the water temperature until she had it right where she wanted it and began filling one of the basins.

She returned to Fig. "I'm going to help you out of your pants," she explained, just like she would to any patient. She undid the button and lowered the zipper. "Bend your knees and lift up," she instructed.

He did. As she slid down his pants, his underwear came, too. Since he didn't seem to have a problem with it, she made sure to maintain his privacy by keeping him covered by the hospital gown. Then she slid both down his long legs, taking his socks with her as she did.

With one basin filled, she began filling the other and returned to the bed. "I'm going to remove your gown now."

Fig lay there with his eyes closed.

She slid the top half off his shoulders and down his arms, leaving it folded over his groin. Then she covered him from his neck to his ankles with towels, laying them crossways, pulling out the gown when she was all done.

When the second basin was filled she moved each to the over-the-bed table, set the height level with the mattress and got to work. "Let me have your left hand," she said. Fig lifted it. His eyes still closed.

Roxie washed his hand and between his fingers. She spent extra time on it because Fig seemed very conscious of the cleanliness of his hands, to the point he carried a hand sanitizer with him. Then she submerged his hand in the rinse basin. "Let it

soak for a minute." In nursing school, while posing as a patient—in her bikini—for the demonstration on bed baths, the teacher had set each of
Roxie's hands to soak in the bathwater. It'd felt so
good Roxie made it a point to do the same for each
of her patients.

"I'm going to start with your head." His beautiful
head. "Lift." She slid a towel beneath it then dipped
the first of her washcloths in the heated water of
the other basin and squeezed out the excess. She
cleansed him gently, carefully. After rinsing his
face and behind his ears, Roxie dipped the cloth in
the clean water, squeezed it until it stopped dripping and set it over his eyes and forehead.

Then she lowered the towel covering his colorful
chest. As she bathed him, she admired the beautiful artwork covering his upper body, all outdoor
landscapes, she realized, which stuck her as odd
for a man who preferred the indoors. She read
the words tattooed in script on scrolls swirling
over the backdrop of lush flowering bushes and
trees, snow-capped mountains and ocean sunsets:
"Nothing can bring you peace but yourself ~ Ralph
Waldo Emerson," over his left pectoral. "Life is a
sum of all your choices ~ Albert Camus," above his

belly button. "To err is human, to forgive divine ~ Anon.," on his left shoulder. "Happiness depends on ourselves ~ Aristotle," on his right shoulder. "You only live once, but if you do it right, once is enough ~ Joe E. Lewis," curved around the outside of his right pectoral.

The proverbs resonated with her. "My favorite words of wisdom are 'Life may not be the party we hoped for, but while we're here we should dance.'"

"Who said it?" Fig asked.

"I have no idea." But that simple sentence had become the basis of her life, the impetus to have fun and find joy when and where she could.

After Roxie dried his torso, she took the lotion she'd left warming in the sink and massaged it into Fig's upper body, avoiding his right forearm. Usually she wore gloves when giving a bed bath. Today she didn't, relishing the smooth curve of each muscle, praying for healing at every raised scar from his painful past.

"Roll onto your left side." She assisted him, positioning his right arm on a pillow and sliding towels underneath him to catch any dripping water.

After bathing, drying and lotioning him, she worked her fingers into his tight muscles.

"That feels so good," Fig said.

Roxie smiled. "That's what I'm aiming for."

When she'd finished with his legs and feet, Roxie couldn't miss the bulge under the towel covering Fig's groin. She dipped a washcloth in the now sudsy water, wrung it out and placed it in his left hand. "You can do between your legs."

At that he opened his eyes. "I've been thinking about what you said earlier. Technically, I'm not your patient so you don't have to worry about adhering to any professional code of ethics."

She knew that, which was why she'd planned a little something special to help alleviate his distress. "I don't?" Roxie asked, knowing exactly where he was headed.

Fig shook his head. "And since we've already had sex, if you were to…let's say…make any sexual advances—which I wouldn't turn down, by the way—they wouldn't be at all inappropriate. In fact they'd be welcomed. Appreciated even." While giving a hand job during a bed bath certainly wasn't nurselike behavior, it could very well fall into the realm of girlfriendlike behavior. At least a dozen times over the years she'd worked at Madrin Memorial she'd walked into a patient's room to find the curtain drawn and the scent of sex heavy in the air.

Men liked it anywhere. Everywhere.

He still had an hour and a half before the earliest possible time the O.R. might call for him. There was plenty of time, but just to be sure… "Exactly what are you asking for, Fig?"

He took her hand and placed it on his erection so there'd be no doubt. "The bath helped. But I still feel wound tight. I want…"

"Something to release the built-up…tension?"

"Yeah." He closed his eyes and guided her hand over the top of the towel, along the length of him, while he lifted his hips into her touch.

"If you wanted to get rid of the towel," he added, "that'd be okay, too."

She smiled, starting to get into the game he played. "What if I don't want to use my hand?" Roxie asked seductively as she moved to the head of the stretcher and bent down close to his lips. "What if I wanted to use my tongue? Would that be okay?"

"Your mouth is perfection," he said, staring up into her eyes.

She dropped down for a kiss. He turned his head.

She connected with his jaw. Again. Strike two. One more time and she'd call him on it. Or did she really want to know the truth? That her mouth was perfect to go down on him, but not good enough to kiss? He wasn't the first guy to avoid kissing her on the mouth. But his refusal hurt more than the others. Because what they had together—while still new—meant more. He meant more.

No. She would not go there. Today she was playing girlfriend.

But deciding not to use her mouth for anything more than talking and eating until he kissed her, she pulled away the towel, reached for the lotion, squeezed and watched ribbons of white cream twirl around his aroused flesh, all engorged and eager for attention.

She didn't make him wait.

When she squeezed her fingers around his thick, firm flesh and slid from the rounded tip down the smooth, impressive length to the bare skin at its base, Fig let out a pleasure-filled groan. A wonderful sound.

"You like?" she asked, knowing the answer.

"Oh, yeah." Having him in her palm felt so good, Roxie almost groaned, too. She moved her hand in long, slow strokes, lubricated by the lotion. The rise and fall of Fig's chest became more rapid, as did his thrusts to meet her.

Fig pulled at the towel covering his chest until it fell to the floor. His nipples beckoned her. Roxie bent to lick one, the roughened texture making her tongue tingle. She sucked it into her mouth. Okay, eating, talking and nipple sucking, but nothing else.

Fig clutched her head and leaned down to kiss the top of it. "I'll make it up to you." He strained against her palm. "Whatever you want, I'll do." He panted into her hair. "Anything. You feel so damn good. I'm going to…"

And with one final push that lifted his hips completely off the stretcher, Fig released all his tension into the towel Roxie had barely managed to toss on top of him.

While she cleaned him, Fig looked completely relaxed, maybe even asleep. His breathing returned to normal. His eyes closed. But when she covered him with fresh toweling and put up the side rails, he reached for her. "I'm going to take a nap." He sounded like he'd already started. "Come lie with me."

"There's not enough room."

He scooted over and patted the space he'd created to his left.

"I don't want to hurt you."

"Honey, I feel so good I am incapable of recognizing pain."

Good.

"Now come. Lie down with me." He yawned. "We hardly got any sleep last night."

She *was* kind of tired.

"Please," he said. "I need to have you close."

Roxie liked to be needed. So she slipped out of her sandals and carefully crawled up beside him. With the utmost care not to jostle his right forearm, she snuggled into his side, her head on his shoulder, her palm over his heart, her knee across his hips. "You comfortable?" she asked.

He nodded. "I like this," he said sleepily. "Just don't try to cook me breakfast," he mumbled.

What? She lifted her head to look at him. He was out.

Roxie closed her eyes, enjoying his strong arm heavy across her back and the tiny twitches as his body fully relaxed in sleep.

While he was in surgery she'd run to visit *Mami*

then make a quick trip to the store for the ingredients to make Mrs. Klein's fabulous chicken soup with matzo balls. Jewish penicillin, she'd called it. Good for whatever ailed you.

Fig was going to love it.

Roxie was in the process of stocking Fig's fridge with food when his cell phone—which she'd held on to along with all of his other valuables when he'd gone up to the O.R.—rang for the third time. She rummaged around her purse until she found it. The screen read: "Mom." Knowing how much her mom worried when she couldn't reach her, Roxie opened the phone. "Hello."

"Who's this?" an older female voice asked.

"Roxie. I'm a friend of Fig's."

"Where is he? What's wrong? Albert," she called out. "Come quick. Something's happened to Ryan."

"He took a little fall. He's in surgery to repair…"

"He's in the hospital," Fig's mother yelled to someone. "Get the car."

"I'm going back to the hospital now. The recovery room called a few minutes ago and said he tolerated the procedure well and should be ready for discharge in a few hours."

"They called you? Why did they call you? I'm his mother. Alllbbbeeerrrttt," she yelled. "Oh, where is that blasted man?" she muttered. "I want to speak to the nurses myself. They need to know Ryan's medical history. He's a very fragile young man."

He didn't seem fragile to Roxie.

"Come. Come. I'm waiting. What hospital is he in?"

"Madrin Memorial." Roxie almost said *ma'am*.

"I'll be there as soon as I can," Fig's mom said.

"You really don't have to…" The connection ended. "I have everything under control," she finished, although no one was there to hear her.

CHAPTER SEVEN

FIG felt absolutely horrible. Out of habit he scanned the recovery room for his mother, which was absolutely ridiculous since she was hours away and had no idea where he was. He retched again. The extra antinausea medication the nurse had shot into him wasn't working. Fig didn't care. "I want to go home," he told the nurse standing beside him, holding the small plastic bowl he was supposed to puke into.

"Not until you're taking oral fluids," she said.

The thought of swallowing anything made him retch again. "You said I could go after I peed." Which he'd done, into a plastic urinal container, with his nurse standing beside him—listening and watching as if he'd planned to substitute someone else's urine for his own. All while his ass hung out from the back opening of his hospital gown. The ultimate humiliation.

She held out a cup of water with a straw in it.

"Once you're drinking I can discontinue your intravenous."

He would never drink that easily contaminated tap-water swill despite the lining of his throat feeling like it'd been impaled with thousands of tiny shards of glass. Fig only drank bottled water. From bottles he opened himself. "I *am* going home," Fig said. "Either discharge me or give me the papers to sign out against medical advice. I'm leaving either way. Where are my clothes?"

"Roxie took them. She said she'd bring you back clean ones to put on."

Damn it. He had to leave now. Before his lungs tightened to the point he could not choke in a breath. Before his eyes blurred and he started to shake. Before the doctor ordered a sedative to drug him into a complacency that would enable people to manipulate him as they pleased.

No. Fig wasn't a scared little boy anymore, and he'd walk out of here half-naked if he had to.

"I'm going to call your doctor," the nurse said in a huff and walked back to the nurses' station.

About a minute later Roxie strolled in with a brightly colored "Feel Better Soon" balloon floating from a red ribbon wrapped around her palm.

"You've got Helen all in a tizzy. For a seemingly laid-back guy, you are one terrible patient." She plopped a grocery bag with his clothes on the foot of his bed.

"Take this out of me, will you?" Fig held up his left arm to show her his IV.

"I'm not on duty, and I'm not your nurse."

Fig tried to pick at the tape, only to find his right hand next to useless.

"Stop that."

Fig looked up at her, waited until her eyes met his so she'd know he was serious. "I am going home." He retched. Damn it.

Roxie grabbed the bowl and thrust it under his chin. He spit.

"He's having a bad reaction to anesthesia." His nurse returned. "Since it's so late, Dr. Rosen wants to admit him overnight."

"I am not staying. Take this out." He held up his left arm. Or he'd find a way to rip it out himself. "You can't keep me here. I know my rights."

His nurse shook her head.

"Tell Dr. Rosen he can release Fig to my care. Ask him to prescribe a couple of Phenergan suppositories."

"I don't need to be released into anyone's care." Just dump him in his bed, let him sleep off this whole experience and he'd be back to normal come morning. Fig slid his legs over the side of the bed and fought against a swirl of dizziness to remain upright.

"Tell me what I need to know," Roxie said to the nurse, who handed her some papers.

"The surgery went well. The splint stays on for seven to ten days. He needs to call Dr. Rosen's office on Monday to schedule his first post-op visit. If all goes well, he'll likely be placed in a hard cast for six weeks." She sorted through the papers she'd handed Roxie and pulled one out. "He needs to begin active digit and shoulder range of motion exercises daily as of tomorrow. This is the instruction sheet. Oral pain medication every four to six hours as needed." The nurse looked at him. "If he can tolerate it."

"Stop talking like I'm not here." He dumped out the bag. Bless Roxie for bringing him sweatpants and a loose tee with big armholes so he could dress himself. He stood. Wobbled.

Roxie caught him up against her. "What's your rush? Got a hot date?"

He flashed her the best smile he could manage considering he felt so crappy. "Smokin' hot," he said, because Roxie was.

"Keep the arm elevated," the nurse went on. "Check nail beds and report any deepening or change in color. Sling with elbow at ninety-degrees flexion. You know all this stuff," she added.

"Yeah, but I want him to hear it." She pivoted Fig back to the bed and he sat. "Is it okay with you if I discontinue the IV?" Roxie asked the nurse.

"Go ahead." The plump woman turned away. "I'll call in for the new med orders."

Roxie removed the annoying tube from his arm and, after applying pressure, put on a gauze-and-tape dressing. "I'll help you get dressed," she offered.

"I don't need help," Fig said. He relied on no one. Trusted no one.

"All righty, then," she said, plopping into the chair facing his bed, leaning back and crossing her legs. "Get to it."

She wasn't going to force her assistance on him or lecture him about accepting help when he needed it? Well, what d'ya know? He decided to put on his pants first. Unfortunately for him, in the aftermath of his surgery and interminable retching, the simple act of untangling his clothing and shaking out his sweatpants tired him out. Pushing through it, he held the waistband in his left hand, leaned forward, planning to thread his feet into the leg holes—and kept on going.

Roxie caught him again. "You keep winding up in my arms and people are going to talk."

She sat him up.

"What do you think they'll say?" he asked, glad she kept the conversation light and casual instead of pointing out how weak and dizzy he was and how ludicrous it was for him to think he could go home on his own.

She knelt on the floor, slid the sweatpants up to his knees and lifted the hems until his feet popped out. Then she stood, hooked both hands under his armpits and helped him stand. "Probably something like, 'What is it about Roxie that even drugged-up post-op patients can't keep their hands—or in your case, hand—off of her?'"

He pulled up his pants with his left hand, dropped back onto the bed and waited for her to comment that he hadn't bothered with the underwear she'd brought for him. She didn't. "I bet they all wish they had your allure." He untied his gown at the neck and took it off. Then he eyed the shirt, trying to decide the best approach to put it on.

She laughed. "Is that what I have?" She stepped between his thighs, picked up the shirt and carefully worked it up his bandaged arm. "Allure?"

"In spades." He looked up at her. Roxie stretched the neck opening over his head. With her help, he pushed his left arm in then pulled the shirt over his belly.

She moved the chair close to the bed and pulled one of his feet into her lap. "You sweet-talker." And without another word, she slid on his sock and sneaker, tied his laces then did the same with the other foot.

The nurse returned. "You need to sign these papers." She pushed them across his over-the-bed table and handed him a pen.

How was he supposed to sign with his left hand? To get out of there, he'd find a way. He picked up the pen. Dropped it. Picked it up again, this time holding it tighter. Then, in a very careful—yet still illegible—attempt at a signature, and without reading a word, Fig signed every place the nurse pointed.

That done, he was free to leave. He went to stand.

"Hold up," Roxie said. "I'm going to run to the pharmacy to get your prescriptions filled, then I'll drive the car around. I'll call up to the nurses' station when I'm ready for you and your nurse will wheel you down."

"I'd rather go with you."

Roxie put her hand on his shoulder. "I know. But it's better if you rest for a few minutes." She plumped his pillow. "Lie back."

He did. Surprised at how good it felt.

"And you really need to try to drink."

His stomach clenched. "Would you pick me up a bottle of water or ginger ale?"

"Sure," she said, without question.

A short time later his nurse pushed him through the electronic doors leading to the outside, and the band of anxiety that'd tightened around his chest since he'd first arrived at the hospital loosened, enabling Fig to inhale a deep breath of fresh air. Freedom.

Roxie got out of her little red car—leaving his balloon floating in the backseat—and walked around the front of it to open the door for him.

A huge silver Mercedes crossover skidded to

a stop, missing Roxie's rear fender by inches. It looked just like… It couldn't be.

His mother climbed out of the front passenger door. How the hell did she…?

"Oh, thank goodness, we're just in time," she yelled. "Wheel him over here. He'll be coming home with us."

"No," Fig said, rage using up what little energy he'd racked up from his rest.

"He doesn't know what he's saying. He's not well. Come. Come." His mother opened the rear door and waited, doing her best Impatient Lady of Power impersonation. His father stood and watched, like he always did, unwilling to make any attempt to control her.

Roxie came to stand beside him.

"What did you do?" he snapped. He didn't have the energy to deal with his mother's relentless efforts to get her way.

"Me?" Roxie asked. "I answered your phone— after the third time it rang in as many minutes, might I add—because I didn't want her to worry that you weren't picking up. I had no idea she'd charge into town and swoop down on us in full motherly dudgeon at the thought of someone else taking care of you."

"Swoop?" his mother said. "I most certainly do not swoop."

"I've got to get back to work," his nurse said. "Pick a car. Either car."

"The red one," Fig said.

"That vile creature must be the girl from the bar," his mother said to his father in a loud whisper audible to everyone within fifty feet of them. The way she said "girl" made her low opinion of the *girl* in question crystal clear.

"Mom," Fig warned.

"Yes," Roxie said, unfazed. "That would be me. The shiksa." She held out her hand to his mother, who now stood within reach. "I go by Roxie."

Fig tried to hide his smile. To his knowledge, his mom had never come across anyone like Roxie before. If he didn't feel so close to passing out he would have sat back and enjoyed the encounter.

His mother looked at Roxie like she had open sores. "What kind of…woman would stand between a mother and her son?" she yelled, clutching at her chest in a performance that garnered the attention of several passersby. "A shameless gold digger," she answered her own question then waited for Roxie's reaction.

"I've been called a lot of things in my day, and I'll cop to the 'shameless,' but 'gold digger' is a new one for me," Roxie said, stepping behind his wheelchair and pushing him toward her car. "You holding out on me, Fig?" She leaned forward to whisper in his ear. "Obviously I've been too free with my favors. From now on I'm going to hold out for some bling."

Only Roxie could make him smile at that precise moment in time.

"His name is Ryan," his mother snapped. "And he is coming home with *me*." She grabbed Roxie's arm.

Roxie stopped. "He's a grown man. Why don't we ask him what he wants to do?" She walked in front of the wheelchair. "Who are you going home with?"

Since neither would have accepted that he wanted to go home alone and all he needed was a ride, Fig said, "You," to Roxie. Then he picked up the plastic bowl in his lap and retched.

"Oh, dear," his mother cried out.

"Get me out of here," he said to Roxie.

"I am a registered nurse, Mrs. Figelstein, so you don't have to worry." Roxie pushed him the rest of the way to her car. "I'll take good care of him." She locked the wheels. "I've discussed the discharge orders with the recovery room nurse. I've picked up his medications, and I'll thank you to remove your hand from my arm so I can assist him into my car without hurting you."

"Where is she taking you, honey?" his mom asked. "I'll come by to get you settled in."

"Go home, Mom."

"I can't believe this," she said dramatically, dabbing at her eyes. "I dropped everything to travel for hours so I could be here to take care of you in your time of need, and you're turning me away?" she sobbed.

"I didn't ask you to come." He didn't want her here, didn't want her anywhere near him when he wasn't operating at full capacity.

"We'll follow you. Get in the car, Albert."

With a steadying hand from Roxie, Fig stood and stared down his mother. "If you come anywhere near where I'm staying, I will cut you out of my life for good. Same rules as my apartment. I mean it."

"It's okay," Roxie said in his ear. "I can handle her."

People only thought they could handle his mother. No one recognized her for the master manipulator she was until it was too late.

"I'll call you tomorrow," Fig said to his mother.

"You always say you'll call, but you never do," his mother countered.

"Because you don't give me a chance to."

"I'll call you tonight. To see if you need anything. We'll find a motel."

"Don't call me tonight because my phone will be off. And don't call me tomorrow because I'm getting a new number and I am not giving it to you."

His mother clutched at her heart again. "Oh, the pain of watching my son turn his back on me. After all I've done for him. My pills, Albert. Where are my pills?"

"Enough," Fig said. "You got me home last weekend with your unnecessary trip to the emergency room. The doctor said you'll outlive us all. Go home, Mom. If I need you, I'll call you."

With one last look at his mother's shocked face, Fig slid into the car, pulled the door closed and relaxed back in his seat.

When Roxie pulled out of the hospital parking lot, she glanced in her rearview mirror. "Woo wee.

I thought for sure they'd follow us and I'd have to show off some of my tricky-bo-dicky driving skills to lose them." She actually sounded a bit disappointed at the missed opportunity. "I think on the scale of one to crazy, I'd rather have an inattentive, introverted, hoarding mother than a manipulative, histrionic, attention-seeking one," Roxie said matter-of-factly as she turned into Kyle's condo complex.

Just like that, at first meeting, Roxie had his mother's true nature pegged. "Neither one is a prize," Fig said, his stomach not feeling so good.

"You got that right," Roxie agreed. "So your mom's the reason you missed our date?"

"Yeah."

"Why didn't you say so?"

"Because I knew it was a ploy to get me home, but I let her suck me in with her tears and her desperate pleas. I was angry at her and myself. I didn't want you to think I was a pansy mama's boy running home every time she called." His stomach clenched. "I think I'm going to be sick." And he was.

Hours later—after he'd waited until his abdominal muscles ached like he'd been beaten and he felt so tired and drained he could barely lift his head—Fig allowed Roxie to give him the nausea medication. He appreciated that she did it quickly and efficiently and without making a big deal out of it. In fact she chattered on about random nothingness the entire time. "You smell like chicken soup," Fig pointed out after she'd finished; the smell not at all appealing.

"That's because while you were in here suffering and not allowing me to do anything for you, I made us a pot of my delicious chicken soup." She stripped off her exam glove and walked to the garbage. "Well, Mrs. Klein's delicious chicken soup. But she wasn't the one who spent the past three hours peeling, stirring and straining it, now, was she?"

Fig retched.

Roxie returned to the bed, sat down and rubbed his back. "The medicine should kick in in a few minutes. Don't worry, I won't force-feed you the soup tonight—even though you're not drinking near as much as you should be. Mrs. Klein always said it needs to sit overnight in the fridge so you can strain the fat in the morning."

At least that'd buy him some time.

"I wish you had asked me first. I don't like chicken soup," he lied. He used to love it until he'd figured out it was one of the many food sources his mother had probably used to poison him.

The next morning Roxie lay in bed listening to Fig's shallow breaths, watching his peaceful expression and relishing the warm, cozy feeling of waking up with him—even though she was the only one awake. She wished she could confide in him and tell him the truth about Johnny and the video. Seek his counsel on what she should do. But regardless of how close they'd become in such a short time, she barely knew him, had no idea how he'd react, and she wasn't ready to give him up. Not yet.

He stirred, gave a tiny stretch and turned onto his side. He'd be up soon. So she quietly slid out of bed and headed to the kitchen to get breakfast started.

So what if he didn't like chicken soup? She liked it. And once upon a time *Mami* had liked it. She could pack some up for Ali and Jared and Victoria and Kyle. It would not go to waste.

But she'd made it for Fig. Making chicken soup

for someone was a labor of love, Mrs. Klein used to say. While Roxie didn't love Fig, he'd been a good friend to her when she'd really needed one. He'd taken down her video. He'd stood up for her to the fire marshal, and he'd given her a place to stay. He'd accompanied her to the hospital— twice—when he hated hospitals. So she wanted to demonstrate her appreciation by doing something special for him. That he didn't like, and didn't even appear interested in tasting, the soup she'd worked so hard on was disappointing.

But it wasn't the first disappointment she'd ever suffered, and most likely would not be the last. Roxie shook it off and opened the fridge. She took out the eggs and milk she'd bought yesterday—because Fig didn't have enough food in his refrigerator to feed a gerbil. She slid two pieces of split-top wheat bread into the toaster—in case all he could stomach was toast—and filled the kettle—in case he felt up to some coffee.

On the chance he was as hungry as she thought he'd be after last night's ordeal, she also got started on making him a nice "thanks for everything, I think you're special" breakfast.

Roxie cracked five eggs into a bowl and took

down the cinnamon and vanilla and found she couldn't stop smiling. She loved playing pretend girlfriend, working in Kyle's bright kitchen cooking for her temporary man. If she'd been able to find a frilly apron in one of the drawers, she would have put it on and danced around—in a room devoid of clutter where she actually had space to prepare a decent meal and had access to pots and utensils without having to search for them.

"Whatever you're doing, stop," Fig commanded from the doorway to the bedroom. "Give me a minute and *I'll* make *you* breakfast."

"Don't be ridiculous," Roxie said. "You've only got one functioning arm and I've got two." She held them up and wiggled her fingers. "Besides, I've already started. Pick your poison. French toast made with delicious challah bread. Eggs. An omelet. Toast. Coffee. Oh, and there's O.J. in the fridge but I wasn't sure if you were a juice drinker in the morning."

He walked to the kitchen, looking tired and perturbed. "I can make my own breakfast," he grumbled.

"Then what's the sense of having *me* here?"

He pulled out a kitchen chair and sat down heavily. "Exactly."

What? "You don't want me here?"

He rubbed his hand over his face. "I can't do this. You insisted on staying last night. But I'm feeling much better this morning."

He didn't look much better. She wiped her hand on a towel. "I thought…" That he liked having her around. That he'd invited her to stay until they were done cleaning out the house. That last night he was just being a difficult patient. "I didn't realize…" That he'd intended for her to stay for only one night. That once they'd had sex he was done with her. Like all the rest of them. "I'll get my things."

"Roxie. Wait."

Absolutely not. She wouldn't stay where she wasn't wanted. But she'd taken responsibility for his care. "Let me see your right hand."

He held it out to her.

"Mild swelling. To be expected. Make sure you keep it elevated." She pinched his nail beds. "Good capillary refill. Move your fingers." He did. "Good range of motion." She turned to the bedroom. Would not get sappy. "Your home exercise plan is on the kitchen counter. Your prescription bottles are by the toaster. Don't forget to call Dr. Rosen's office to schedule your post-op visit."

"I'm sorry," he said.

And Roxie snapped. "Do you have any idea how many times you've apologized to me in the last forty-eight hours?"

He didn't answer.

"Way more than someone who wants to be my *friend* should have to. But you're not interested in being friends, are you? No. You got what you wanted and now I'm being sent on my way."

"Sorry," a different male voice said.

Kyle stood at the front door, his key still in the lock, starring at Fig's shirtless torso. "You showed her your tattoos?"

"Don't you knock?" Fig asked.

"I came to check on you. I didn't think you'd let Roxie…" Kyle stopped.

"Don't worry about it," Roxie said to Kyle. "I have just been informed I've overstayed my welcome. I'll be gone in a few minutes."

"It's not like that," Fig said, his voice now an annoying buzzing in her ears.

"Where will you go?" Kyle asked.

At least one of them cared enough to ask. "I've got plenty of options," Roxie said. Although she didn't want to bother anyone, so probably a motel. Something cheap, since there was a good chance she would soon be unemployed.

"Since we expect your mom will be moving into the downstairs bedroom this afternoon, you can have Victoria's couch." He looked semihopeful.

Roxie smiled. "She didn't agree to let you share the master bedroom, after all."

Kyle shook his head. "Not unless Jake has a sleepover. But if you were to need the couch…"

"She'll probably send you here to sleep with Fig," Roxie said. "Victoria's mind is set. She doesn't want Jake to see his parents sleeping in the same bed until after you're married. There's no getting around it."

Roxie's mind was set, too. "I need to get my things." She turned and pounded down the hall to the bedroom. How could she have misread Fig? She picked up her bag from the floor and dropped it onto the bed. How could she have gotten so caught up in playing pretend girlfriend? Which, for a very short, very emotional twenty-four hours, had started to feel all too real. She put on a pair of denim capri pants, tied the T-shirt she'd worn to bed at her low back and slipped into her flip-flops.

She grabbed her watch from the table beside the bed and her lip gloss from the dresser beneath the mirror, and she was ready to go.

"You're being an idiot," Kyle yelled at Fig. "Roxie is my friend, and she deserves an explanation. Tell her. Or I will."

"Tell me what?" Roxie entered the open kitchen.

"Nothing," Fig said to Roxie. Then he stood and faced Kyle. "Don't do this."

"You care about her," Kyle said to Fig.

Seems he'd misread Fig, too.

"I can see this is ripping you apart," Kyle said.

That's when Roxie noticed how tormented and sad and downright distraught Fig looked. But he was the one who'd told her to go.

"Don't let her leave," Kyle went on. "Take a chance. Talk to her. Let her make her own choice."

Kyle walked to Roxie and eased the strap of her bag off of her shoulder. "Hear him out, Roxie. You will never find a better, more loyal and supportive man." He hugged her and whispered in her ear, "The good outweighs the inconvenient. I promise you."

His words made no sense.

Kyle walked to the door and set Roxie's bag beside it. "I'm leaving now. But I'll be waiting in the parking lot." He looked at Fig. "If Roxie leaves this apartment in less than fifteen minutes I am going to come back up here and beat you senseless."

"Oh, you think so?" Fig asked in honest challenge. "Even one-handed I can take you."

"So you'd rather fight than take a few minutes to tell me what's going on?" Roxie asked quietly.

Kyle escaped through the door and clicked it closed behind him.

"I'm a kook," Fig said. "A nut job."

"If you're trying to scare me into leaving, you'll have to do better than that." Roxie leaned a shoulder against the wall and crossed her arms at her waist, not knowing what else to do with them.

"You've got so much going on in your life right now. You deserve an easy man, not someone like me."

"I've never had easy a day in my life. I wouldn't know what to do with an easy man."

"In that case, can I make you some coffee?" Fig asked.

"I'm still trying to decide if I should stay or if I

should let you get beat up," Roxie said, only half kidding. "So answer me this. Is Kyle right? Do you care about me? Is the thought of me walking out that door ripping you apart?"

Fig looked down at the floor and nodded.

Roxie's heart felt a tiny bit hopeful. "Then I'll make the coffee."

"No." Fig lifted the kettle in his left hand and walked to the sink.

"That's fresh water," Roxie said. "I filled it this morning."

Fig dumped it out, struggled to dry the inside with paper towels and refilled it using three containers of bottled water—that were not easy for him to open one-handed. But he didn't ask for help and Roxie didn't offer. He glanced at her on the way to the stove, his expression a mix of uncertainty and embarrassment.

"Does this all have to do with your frequent hand washing/sanitizing and why you won't kiss me?"

He rested his hip against the counter. "Noticed that, did you?"

"I'm a nurse. I have excellent assessment skills." Roxie walked to the cabinet where she'd seen the coffee mugs and took two down. Then she got two spoons from the silverware drawer.

Fig watched her every move.

"You going to answer me?" Roxie asked.

"It's indirectly related." He reached into a cabinet and took out individual-serving-size packets of instant coffee. He held them out to Roxie. "Would you…?"

She washed her hands in the sink then ripped the tops off the coffee packets.

"There's milk in the…"

Fig held out a handful of single-serving creamers.

Roxie peeled back the lids on four of them.

"Thank you," Fig said.

The coffee made, they both sat down at the table.

"The no kissing on the mouth, and the hand washing—which is not a compulsion, I'd like to point out… It's not like I scrub my hands raw, or anything. I just like them to be clean—started back when I was first diagnosed with leukemia. My mother lectured me on the risk of infection and how to protect against it. Constantly. For years. It is now hardwired into my circuitry."

"And you can put your tongue between my legs

but not between my lips." She hesitated, thought about what she'd said and clarified, "These lips," while pointing to her mouth.

"It's a conundrum." He smiled and shrugged. "Can't explain it."

"So you're a selective germaphobe. That's the big secret?"

Fig stirred his coffee. "Have you ever heard of Munchausen syndrome by proxy?"

"Isn't it a form of child abuse?"

"It can affect adults, too. It occurs when an abuser, usually a mother, intentionally harms or fabricates an illness in her child that initiates a hospitalization."

There were some sick people in the world. "Are you trying to tell me your mother somehow convinced your doctors that you had leukemia when you didn't? Because I'm not buyin' it."

He shook his head. "No. I definitely had the leukemia. But during my remissions I suffered from debilitating headaches and forgetfulness and general malaise to the point I didn't feel well enough to leave the house. No one could identify a reason. Mom homeschooled me. Her life revolved around me, her every waking hour dedicated to me. She carted me to doctors and specialists. I underwent countless tests. All the while she soaked in the praise for what a wonderful, attentive mother she was, giving up her life to care for her sick son."

He stared into his coffee as he spoke. Roxie felt sorry for little Fig, sick, so alone and subjected to a controlling mother. But Munchausen by proxy was a hefty accusation.

"By the time I'd turned eighteen—" Fig took a sip of coffee and continued "—I was clinically depressed. Living at home. I had more bad days than good, and I couldn't visualize my future being anything but more of the same. One night I drank more of my dad's stash of expensive beer than usual and got totally wasted. Jacked up on liquid confidence, I stole the family Ford and, while speeding down the highway, decided to take control of my life...by ending it."

Roxie couldn't believe it. This strong, confident man had attempted suicide? As bad as things had gotten in her life, she'd never once considered it. "Your accident. The one you told me about." The one that'd left him scarred.

"Wasn't an accident at all."

"Oh, Fig. I'm so sorry."

"I'm not." He stared off into the living room. "I met Kyle in rehab and he saved my life, although it took him almost losing his to do it. I remember Mom coming into our room late one night. She'd befriended the staff, bribed them with cookies and treats and wasn't held to the same rules as other visitors. I heard her out in the hallway and pretended to be asleep—I did that a lot so she'd leave me alone. Anyway, she came in close to my bed and whispered, 'I'm so sorry, Ryan. I never expected it to go on this long, to make you so unhappy. It was selfish. I'll stop. I promise.'"

"What?"

"It didn't make sense to me at the time, either. But after Kyle's brush with death, when we sat down to try to make sense of what'd happened, I remembered Mom's words and the pieces of the puzzle started to come together."

"What happened to Kyle?" Roxie asked.

"Sorry," Fig said. "I got ahead of myself. In rehab, Kyle and I hit it off right from the start. I know it sounds pathetic, but he was my first real friend."

Roxie reached for his unbandaged hand and

squeezed. For as difficult as her childhood had been, Fig's was worse.

"Long story short, after rehab and some convalescence at my house, my father got us both into the same college and we moved into an apartment close to campus. Mom was not happy about me moving out and refused to allow me to live in the dorms. Too many germs, she'd said. An apartment was the compromise."

"Sounds like an eighteen-year-old's dream, to be set up in an apartment with his buddy." Roxie would have loved an opportunity like that.

"It was. Until Mom started visiting. Daily. For hours at a time. She insisted on cleaning the apartment, doing our laundry and cooking for us. Kyle's mom had died a few years earlier and he didn't mind the attention as long as she was gone right after she did the dinner dishes."

"How long did she give you on your own before she started coming around?" Roxie asked.

"About a month. In that time I'd started to feel better." His face lit up at the memory. "Up until that point, it's the happiest I'd ever been. I had friends and went on dates. Then the headaches and nausea started up again. I began missing class.

Mom suggested I move home but I refused. The symptoms got worse."

"You didn't relate the change in your health to your mom's visits?"

He looked up at her. "It was par for the course for me. I'd never gone more than a few weeks without relapsing. To be honest, I expected it."

"So what made you suspect your mom?"

"One weekend Kyle was up late studying. Mom had made us each a batch of brownies. She always packaged them separately, saying mine had herbs and supplements to help me get well, and while I was used to the slight change in taste—because she'd been giving them to me for years—Kyle might find the taste off-putting. But that particular night Kyle was so munched he didn't care. He devoured my pan of brownies. About three-quarters of the batch. In one sitting. An hour later he collapsed in my room and had a seizure."

CHAPTER EIGHT

"Ay Dios mio," Roxie said.

Fig remembered that horrible night, the fear and desperation, waiting for the ambulance and not knowing what to do. "The emergency room doc said Kyle demonstrated signs of acute poisoning. But they couldn't identify the source. They pumped his stomach and gave him all sorts of medication." Fig had broken down and cried with relief when, after hours of treatment, the doctor finally told him Kyle would be okay. "When he got well he was convinced there was something wrong with the brownies."

"Maybe he had a bad reaction to one of the supplements your mom added."

Fig had suggested the same thing. But, "He didn't exhibit signs of allergic reaction. The doctor was very clear. He suspected poisoning by an unidentified agent."

"But you ate the brownies. How come you weren't affected?"

"I'm not big on sweets. Mom knew that. I'd have one, maybe two small brownies a day. I usually wound up throwing half of them out because they got stale before I finished them."

"I can't believe it," Roxie said. "What kind of mother would poison her son's brownies?"

"One desperate for attention and validation. One desperate to be needed. My dad traveled a lot. Even when he was home he spent most of his time on the phone or relaxing in his den. And it wasn't just my brownies. Looking back, I remembered the drops I'd caught her putting in my soup one time, and my water glass another. 'Homeopathic remedies,' she'd said."

"And now you won't eat soup, and you'll only drink bottled water."

If only that were the extent of it. "It goes beyond that, Roxie. My mother, the woman who was supposed to love me more than anyone, the woman I trusted to care for me, who I'd thought wanted only the best for me, poisoned my food. For years. With the intent to make me sick."

"How do you know for sure? Did you confront her?"

Of course he had. "She denied it. To this day she insists she never gave me anything but what my doctors prescribed and recommended. I asked to see the bottles of the homeopathic preparations and herbs she'd added to my food. She came up with excuse after excuse. I searched for them, and never found one."

"Maybe…"

No. There were no maybes. "Within a week or two of removing every item of food she either made for me or bought for me from our apartment, and taking control of what I ate and where it came from, I began to feel healthy and strong. I know, in here—" he raised his fist to his heart "—that she did it. You saw how she is. Conniving. Manipulative. What's to stop her from trying again? What's to stop someone else from slipping something in my food for any number of reasons?"

"Do you honestly think I'm the type of person who would poison your food?"

"I know, I sound insane, and what I have going on is not rational, but I refuse to lose one more day of my life because I feel too sick to go out and live it."

Roxie took a sip of coffee. "Have you talked to anyone about all this?"

"Kyle. And now you."

"I mean a professional."

He smiled. "I know. And no, I haven't."

"Maybe it's time you did. Because your issues with food obviously bother you to the point you're trying to hide them. In my opinion you've transferred control of your life from your mother to your irrational fear of being poisoned."

How the heck did she read people and situations so quickly and thoroughly and correctly?

"You know, I've got to tell you, we all have issues, Fig. You're really not all that special. Unless there's something else? Something that might crop up later tonight or tomorrow and have you wanting to get rid of me again?"

"No. And I didn't *want* to get rid of you. I thought…"

"Well, you may change your mind when you learn I don't like anyone to touch my belly button. I avoid foods with artificial red coloring and artificial sweeteners. I am fanatic about keeping my immediate living area spotless. And I have a thing about organization—especially in my closet."

"I can live with that." As long as she could put up with him. Please let her be willing to at least try.

"Now just so I'm sure I understand, I can stay here as long as I don't mess with your food or try to cook for you?"

"Yes."

"Do you have any problem cooking for me?"

"No."

She walked to the door, picked up her bag and turned toward the bedroom. "Good. You feel up to making French toast?"

He smiled. "Sure."

"Thanks. I'm going to jump in the shower."

That was it. Done. Fig blew out a relieved breath. He'd shared his biggest secrets, and rather than bolting for the door, Roxie responded by asking him to make French toast while she went to take a shower. Granted, he'd known her for only less than two weeks, and they'd gotten off to a rather rocky start, but her actions affirmed what Fig was starting to feel in his heart. Roxie had definite long-term potential.

Did she have any idea how special she was?

So different from all the other women he knew. Accepting. Honest. Roxie said what was on her mind and went after what she wanted. She played at tough but turned out to be sensitive and caring. She understood him and knew what he needed before he did. Fig could read her, too. He'd hurt her this morning. Roxie deserved better.

Before he could think better of it, determined to make amends, he had his right arm sealed in plastic wrap and was pushing open the bathroom door.

"You can't get that arm wet," Roxie cautioned as soon as he entered.

The fact that she didn't tell him to let her shower in peace was as good as an invitation. Fig dropped his boxers and pushed back the shower curtain.

"Oy," Roxie said in the process of rinsing shampoo from her hair, rivulets of suds streaming down her firm, tan, luscious body. Fig went from semi-erect to full-on let's-get-busy. "In order to stay here I have to put up with your freaky eating habits *and* have sex with you? It's too much. What's in it for me?"

That was the problem with not thinking a plan all the way through. No protection. Fig climbed into the tub anyway, holding his right arm up and away from the spray of the shower, and closed the curtain behind him. "I'll feed you well and give you lots of orgasms." He hooked his left arm behind her back and pulled her front flush with his.

Roxie wrapped her arms around his neck and rubbed her warm, slippery, magnificent body from side to side, her taut nipples scraping across his chest, her pelvis cradling him, her bare mons igniting his fire.

She kissed his neck. "Works for me. What do you get out of it?"

He hugged her close. "You." Day and night, to cuddle up to in his bed and brighten his wide-awake hours.

"Smart man. I can be very useful to have around," she said enticingly.

Of that he had no doubt.

"I can help you with your shower, for instance." She stepped away, picked up the soap and nestled it between her palms. She stroked it and twirled it sensually until a foamy lather seeped between her fingers.

Fig's erection envied that soap, wanted to be that soap. He swallowed. "You have an uncanny ability to know exactly what I need." When Roxie set her sudsy hands to his chest, his man-parts sent out a flare of excitement that left behind a residual intense yearning. His body throbbed with a desire only Roxie could satisfy.

From his neck down her soft hands left no part of him untouched, her movements more graceful and arousing than purposeful. The experience: incredible. The end result: one clean, ready-for-sex man.

"I think you should get another tattoo," Roxie said. "Around here." She drew a circle on his thigh. "An itty-bitty raccoon."

Tease. He pulled her close, ran his hand down her back and squeezed her right butt cheek. "How about you get one right here? To give me something to spank."

She actually trembled. Fig had never even considered spanking a woman prior to Roxie, had never been as scared and angry as she'd made him the night of the fire. But if she liked it he'd do it. Anything to please her.

"Rinse," she said.

He stepped beneath the warm water.

Roxie joined him, kissed his shoulder, his chest. "I am in love with your body." She accepted him. As is. Tattoos and quirks and all. It was time to show her how much that meant, how much he was starting to care for her.

"If I had two working hands, this is when I'd pick you up, slam your back to the wall and drive myself deep inside you."

"Ooohhh. Something to look forward to," she said as she took him into her hand and began a slow, sensual glide up and down his swollen shaft. It felt so good. She felt so good. Her long, thin fingers surrounding him, squeezing him, pushing him closer to the edge of ecstasy.

"But you need to take it easy," she said. "Let me do all the work." She went down on her knees.

"No," Fig said, reaching for her with his left hand and helping her up. "Today is all about you."

He closed the distance between them and pressed her back to the center wall, keeping his left side under the water. "Lift this leg." He tapped her right thigh. "Now wrap it around my waist. Open for me. Good girl."

He thrust along the seam of her sex, teasing and titillating, giving her a sample of what was to come. Roxie's breathing became deeper, her movements urgent. She rubbed his head, kissed his cheek, his chin and bottom lip.

Where normally he would have turned his head, Fig froze, waited to see what she'd do next.

"I want to kiss you in the worst way," she said, tracing his bottom lip with her finger.

Deep down he wanted her to kiss him. Wanted to kiss her. But when it came to actually doing it… he couldn't.

"Would it help if I told you I flossed, brushed my teeth and gargled before I got into the shower?" she asked.

In anticipation he'd join her? He leaned back and raised an eyebrow in question.

She nodded. "You, my friend, have a plethora of oral hygiene paraphernalia."

He liked a clean, healthy, as-germ-free-as-he-could-get-it mouth. He stared at her lips, wondered what they'd feel like pressed to his, what she'd taste like. His mom's words haunted him. *The human mouth is the dirtiest part of the body. It contains more germs than a toilet seat. Germs will kill you, Ryan. No kissing on the lips. Ever.*

Damn her. The last thing Fig wanted to think about when he looked at Roxie's beautiful lips was a toilet seat.

"Do you remember yesterday, on the stretcher

in the E.R.?" She rocked along his length, ran her fingertips up and down his sides.

He nodded, although she made it difficult to think about anything other than her hands on his body and how much he wanted to get inside of her, to pleasure her over and over.

"When you said you'd make it up to me? Whatever I want, you'll do? Anything, you said."

Uh-oh. Fig swallowed, knew where this was headed.

"Well, I sure would like it if you'd kiss me."

Ka-pow! *Take that,* arousal. Dread replaced his elation of a moment ago. What woman would appreciate a man experiencing dread at the thought of kissing her? It wasn't normal. It made no sense. He knew that. But still… Now she'd get angry. She had every reason to. He was a mental case. He couldn't look at her. He stepped away and gave her room to leave.

"Hey," she said softly as she took his arm and brought him back to her. "If you're not ready, that's okay. I can wait, but not too long." She lifted his chin. His eyes met hers, soft and caring. "Promise me you'll work on it. To surprise me."

"I will." He buried his face in her neck. Thankful.

Blessed to be with Roxie, who didn't make unrealistic demands and carry on when he couldn't meet them, who simply stated what she wanted, prepared to wait. He would reward her patience with the most amazing kiss ever. Hopefully. After he received some counseling. Which he would inquire about first thing Monday morning. For Roxie. For himself. For a future he'd never thought possible before today.

"I'm sorry I brought it up." She hugged him. "Can we get back to the celebration-of-me day?"

Of course they could. After he took care of a few small details. "You soak for a little while longer. Give me five minutes to get ready," Fig said. He whispered in her ear, "Then dry off and meet me in my bedroom, where we will commence with the Day of Roxie revelry." He kissed her temple. "Come as you are."

Okay. So when the idea of making their next few hours extraordinary and worthy of standing out above every other sexual encounter from Roxie's memory had popped into Fig's head, he'd failed to consider he had only one usable hand.

When Roxie exited the bathroom in full goddess-like nakedness—in way less than the five minutes he'd requested—he'd barely managed to get the bottom sheet on the bed.

"Mocha satin," she said, rubbing the still-folded top sheet against her cheek. "These things are legit. Me likey." She took over making the bed and winked. "Conserve your first-day-post-op energy. You're going to need it." She had the bed made in minutes.

He glanced at the candles he'd placed on each nightstand. Without being asked, Roxie lit them while he closed the blackout curtains.

"You're going all out," Roxie said.

"You're worth it," Fig responded. And she was. Even if she didn't realize it. "Now lie down."

Roxie folded down the top sheet, crawled to the center of the queen-size bed—giving him a tantalizing view of her nice, round posterior—and lay down on her back. "This feels rather decadent." She eyed him askance. "But a party of one is no party." She patted the bed beside her.

Even though the room wasn't completely dark, the light from the candles danced on her beautiful skin. She looked like a serving of rich caramel cream piped onto a bar of mocha chocolate. Fig's mouth watered. Come to find out, he had a sweet tooth, after all.

He grabbed a strip of condoms from the drawer by the bed and held them out to Roxie. "You're in charge."

She scooted to the edge of the bed, eagerly ripped one open and rolled it on. Fig called on every bit of control he possessed to keep himself from tackling her and giving it to her hard and fast. "On your back," he said. "Arms over your head."

Roxie did as instructed because the command in his tone excited her. She settled onto the silky sheets and reached her arms—and what the heck, her legs, too—toward each corner of the bed. Spread out, exposed and open, she was his for the taking.

He watched her, a hint of domination in his gaze. Power.

And with no more than that look, Roxie's body heated and made itself ready to accept him.

"Tell me what you want," Fig said, still standing at the side of the bed.

She wanted him to tie her arms and legs in this

exact position, to do wicked things that would make her scream out with pleasure. "You. I want you."

He joined her on the bed, careful of his right arm. At one point he winced.

"Are you sure you're up for this?" Roxie asked.

Fig settled on top of her, balancing his weight on his left elbow. He stared deeply into her eyes and slid the broad tip of his erection along her warm, wet path. All the way down then back up. Over and over. "I am definitely up for this."

Well, then, let's get started. Roxie tilted her pelvis, hoping with his next pass he'd slide inside.

He didn't.

"Have I told you how beautiful you are?" he asked instead.

She wasn't. Her face was too narrow, her eyes too prominent and her nose resembled a hawk's beak.

"You have the prettiest eyes. When I look into them I can tell exactly what you're thinking."

Oh, no, he couldn't.

And still staring down at her, he thrust deep. Filled her. Touched a part of her she didn't know existed until that very moment, making sex with Fig so much more than a mere physical encounter.

He pulled out and pushed in again. "Today is all about you." Out. In. "Tell me what you want, Roxie." Out. In. "What you *really* want."

She couldn't. Not yet. But there was one thing. "Make love to me." Not down-and-dirty-fill-me-drill-me sex. But slow, sweet, you're-worth-a-little-time-and-effort sex. The kind two people who cared about more than each other's bodies had. It'd be nice to experience that at least once.

Fig got an odd look on his face.

Roxie went hot with embarrassment. "Don't panic. I'm not saying I love you or anything." But if she let herself, she could. Oh, so easily. "I hardly know you."

"Yet you know more about me than friends I've had for years."

She liked knowing his secrets. If only she could share all of hers.

"You can," he said.

"Can what?" Roxie asked.

"Tell me whatever it is you're hiding."

How could he possibly…?

"When you're ready." He kissed her forehead. "Keeping secrets is going to give you wrinkles."

Roxie focused on relaxing her facial muscles. No

stress or indecision or guilt here. "Are we going to spend our day talking? Because there are other things…"

"Wrap your legs around my hips."

Gladly.

He twirled the knuckles of his right hand around her nipple until it tightened into a hard, ticklish peak, and increased his thrusts. The nurse part of her wanted to tell him he shouldn't be using his right hand. The aroused woman part—who loved how he made her feel—took the nurse by the throat and squeezed so not even a peep of sound could escape.

"I wish I had two good hands so I could do everything I want to do to you."

"Improvise," Roxie suggested.

Fig lowered his mouth to her ear. "I'm going to make you love me, Roxie," he whispered, his breath hot and heavy, his hips rocking into her.

He wouldn't have to work hard. It would take far more effort for her to make herself not fall in love with him. "Oh, you think so?" she asked, meeting each thrust.

He bent his knees, shifted up and drove into her, gliding along the exact spot that drove her wild.

"I know so." He lavished attention on the tiny cove at the base of her ear and Roxie reveled in the sensation of having each of her turn-on triggers engaged at the same time.

Soon they were both breathing too heavily to talk. They spoke with their bodies in a mix of tender touches and loving caresses. They communicated via escalating moans, desperate groans and deep, lingering sighs. Roxie had her legs clamped around him, urging him deeper—as if it were even possible.

Then he did something that sent a surge of wonderfulness loose inside of her and Roxie screamed out, "Just like that. Don't stop. Don't you dare stop."

Like he'd hit her power boost she thrust harder, moved faster, and squeezed him tighter than she'd thought herself capable. In return he thrust harder, moved faster and squeezed her tighter right back.

A few minutes later, lying replete on Fig's muscled chest while he twirled his fingers in her hair, unable to move more than her mouth, Roxie said, "We sure are well matched in the bedroom."

Fig kissed the top of her head. "It's a start."

* * *

On Sunday morning Roxie finished wiping the counters with a paper towel and said, "Sit. You made breakfast. I clean up. Then I've got to go."

Fig pulled out a chair, sat down and studied her like he could tell she was hiding something. "What's on the schedule for today?"

"*Mami* made a list of things she wants me to bring over to Victoria's. After I stop by her room to pick it up I need to meet with Victoria to discuss my job and, if I still have one, to put in a request for some more time off." And pick up what she needed for Tuesday night. An ominous feeling of doom weighed heavily on her shoulders. She turned her back to Fig so he wouldn't see.

She hated not being totally honest with him. But he'd never approve, would no doubt want to be involved somehow and he wasn't up to it. As much as she didn't want him to know the truth, she worried about him, too. He looked absolutely drained from them spending the better part of the past twenty-four hours in bed. Not sleeping. Barely resting. They'd been insatiable for each other. He needed to relax and strengthen. Not worry about her. No. She'd handle it herself and put the ordeal behind her. Without Fig ever finding out.

"Then I'm going to the house to try to find everything," she said with forced vigor. "Then it's back to the hospital to wait for *Mami*'s discharge, and a trip to Victoria's to get her settled in."

"I'll come with you," Fig offered.

Any other time she would have taken him up on his offer. She liked having him around. But not today. "Don't be ridiculous." She washed the last of their silverware and set them in the dish rack to dry. "You need to elevate your arm and rest today. But thank you." She walked over to kiss the top of his head. "Really. I appreciate the offer. Now what do you need me to do for you before I go?"

"Leave me your brothers' names, addresses and phone numbers."

"Yeah. About that." She ran the ends of the scarf she'd chosen as a belt through her fingers. "They're not going to come." They didn't care about her or *Mami* one bit. "And they probably won't appreciate you bothering them." And would be obnoxiously vocal about it, like they were back when she used to call them to ask them to come home.

He stood up and slid a pad and pen across the counter. "Names, addresses and phone numbers. You let me handle the rest."

"I don't…" How embarrassing to admit the only number she knew for certain was Ernesto's. While *Mami* wrote down the return addresses from the occasional Christmas cards she received, Roxie couldn't say for certain where any of her brothers lived.

As if he understood he tapped the pad and said, "Write down as much as you know."

"Your time would be better spent sleeping." She did as he asked. "Or preparing me a gourmet dinner."

Fig approached her with his arms open. She stepped between them and he hugged her close. "It's going to be fine, Roxie. They'll come. I'll make it happen."

Roxie pulled back to look at him. "What are you up to?" She studied his face, trying to find the answer. But he gave nothing away.

"It's better you don't know," he teased. "What time do you think you'll be home?"

Home. It would be so nice if this really were her home, and whenever she returned to it, Fig would be there waiting for her, making her feel safe and cared about. Happy.

But she was the pretend girlfriend, and he was

her temporary man. Because *Mami* couldn't live alone, and as soon as her house was habitable, they'd both be moving back into it. And because Fig wasn't the only one with quirks he didn't want others to know about.

"I'll call you and let you know," Roxie answered.

"Call Kyle's house phone. My cell's turned off."

"Did you call your mom?" Roxie asked. She'd already spoken with hers, twice.

"I will," Fig said. "Later."

Roxie detached his cell phone from the charger and handed it to him. "Do it now. So she doesn't worry."

He put the phone down. "She'll worry no matter what."

"Did you ever think maybe if you called her on a regular basis and involved her in your life a bit more she wouldn't call you constantly or go to such extreme lengths to see you?"

Based on his expression, no, he hadn't.

"Either you forgive her for the past or you don't. Either she's in your life or she isn't. All or nothing. Anything less will be a stressor to you both. She'll always be seeking more of your time and attention. And you'll constantly be trying to put her off and make her go away."

"Short of moving back in with her, I'm not capable of giving her the amount of my time and attention she wants."

"Discuss it with her," Roxie suggested. "Set limits. But you'll have to give a little, too."

Fig stared down at the phone in his hands. "Do you think I'm crazy?" He looked up and smiled. "Maybe I should clarify. Crazy for forgiving her?"

"Honestly?"

Fig nodded.

"I don't think you have forgiven her. I think there's part of you that wants to, but a bigger part is still angry and hurt. And unsure. Because you never found out for certain if she purposely set out to hurt you."

"She was a good mom," Fig said. "She used to play with me for hours and read to me. Sing to me." His words drifted off as he remembered something. "She stayed with me and held my hand and refused to leave me alone through countless scary and painful procedures and tests. The leukemia was very real and we battled it for years. Without her, I think I would have given up. Yet she pro-

longed my suffering, to control my life. How am
I supposed to deal with that?"

"You close the door on it and lock it away." Like
she'd chosen to do with all the ways her mother
had failed her. "Or you work things out with your
mom." Roxie kissed his head. "If you want to move
forward and heal, you need to choose."

On Tuesday night Roxie sat at the corner of the bar
at O'Halloran's, praying the pain medication she'd
convinced Fig to take after a particularly—purposely—energetic round of demanding sex kept
him sound asleep for the time it would take her to
accomplish her task and return to him.

"The usual to start?" Triple B asked.

Roxie nodded. He returned with an ice cold bottle of beer.

While she waited, she sipped the familiar brew
to calm her nerves, she listened to the same old
songs playing on the jukebox and watched the reg-
ulars drinking what they typically drank and doing
what they typically did.

But for Roxie, tonight was no ordinary night at
O'Halloran's.

"Well, well, well. If it isn't Roxie Loves Coxie."

His voice grated on her self-control, and she briefly considered breaking her beer bottle over his head. But then she wouldn't get what she needed, and he wouldn't pay for what he'd done, so she lifted it and took a sip of its bubbly goodness instead.

"Fancy meeting you here," he continued the charade.

As if their "date" hadn't been prearranged. "Hi, there, Johnny." She wondered if that was his real name. "Nice to see you again." The remnants of that lie sat bitter on her tongue. But— Nothing to see here, folks. Just two old…friends meeting up for a drink.

As if on cue Triple B meandered over. "What'll you have?" He tossed a napkin on the bar in front of Johnny.

"A beer. Same as her."

Johnny leaned in to whisper in Roxie's ear. The stubble on his cheek grazing hers made Roxie cringe. She much preferred Fig's smooth skin. "Too bad we got all this bad business between us," he said. "We were good together. Had us some fun."

So she'd thought. Until the call she'd hoped was for a second date turned out to be for the purposes of blackmailing her. "You've got yourself some talent," she said.

"Maybe when this is all done we could…"

Not even if someone were holding a loaded gun to her head. "Maybe," she lied. Play the role. Draw him in. Get him talking. "Was it your buddy who filmed us?"

He nodded.

Come on. Talk. "I heard his breathing on the tape." His heavy, excited breathing.

"He likes to watch." Johnny smiled.

"If you'd let me know you were making a video of us, he could have come out of his hidey-hole and gotten closer to the action. I bet he would have liked that." The creeper.

"You mean you would have been okay with it?"

Perfect. "I might have been. If you'd asked real nice."

"I'll keep that in mind for next time."

You do that, scuz-bucket. "So where is he? Your friend."

"He's around."

Roxie scanned the bar, didn't see him.

Triple B delivered Johnny's drink, placing it on the bar with a bit more force than necessary.

Johnny, however, was too busy staring at Roxie's cleavage in the low-cut blouse she'd purposely worn to notice Triple B's bulging biceps and step-out-of-line-and-I'll-beat-you-into-a-coma scowl. Roxie motioned her friend away.

"So you called this meeting, doll. What's up?" Johnny took a swig of beer.

Roxie leaned in close. "I pulled the switch," she said quietly. "The drugs for the tape. That was the deal."

Johnny looked around. "I heard you've been on vacation this week." He eyed her suspiciously.

"One of my best friends is the head nurse on 5E. I dropped in to visit her. She got called out on an emergency, asked me to give her keys to the charge nurse. I saw my opportunity and I took it. Since I wasn't on the schedule to work, if someone figures it out, there's no way they'll trace the switch to me."

Johnny smiled. "Smart girl. I knew from the moment we met you were perfect for the job." He ran a callused finger up and down her arm. "We could make a good team, you and me. In *and* out of the sack."

Roxie fought the revulsion of this man's touch

and sat perfectly still. That he actually thought she was okay with being taken advantage of, videotaped and threatened with exposure. "Did you bring the tape?" Roxie asked.

Johnny nodded. "Just like you asked." He didn't offer any further information. He finished his beer and ordered another—for each of them.

Roxie didn't have time for this. She needed to get the tape and get the heck out of there. "Where is it?"

"My car."

Not the car. Triple B would totally freak if she got up to leave the bar with Johnny. "Ask your friend to bring it in." Then she'd have them both in the same place.

"What's your rush?" Johnny chugged from his second beer. "Drink up."

Roxie lifted her second "beer" to her lips. Triple B had replaced it with ginger ale, like she'd asked. She couldn't risk anything dulling her senses. "I've got a friend waiting on me," she lied.

"The pale, bald guy?"

So he *had* been watching her. "Yeah."

"He your boyfriend?"

"Patient," she answered, wanting to keep Johnny

interested until they'd finished their transaction. "Friend of the family. So. We going to make the exchange or what? I've got to get back before he wakes up."

Johnny finished his beer. "Outside."

She grabbed her purse and stood. What else could she do? Halfway to the door Triple B bellowed, "Where you going, Roxie?"

She plastered a smile so he wouldn't know just how nervous she was. "Outside for a few minutes. I'll be back in to settle up."

"I left enough money for both of us," Johnny said.

Lord help her.

"Five minutes, Roxie." Triple B picked up his wooden drunk-slugger and slammed it down on the bar. "Or I'm coming out after you."

"That was quite a show," Johnny said when they reached the parking lot.

Fear crept up Roxie's spine. Had he figured her out?

Johnny laughed. "But you look like you can take care of yourself."

She almost collapsed with relief. "He worries. I went to school with his wife."

Johnny walked past car after car. She'd been so drunk the night they'd left together she had no recollection of what he'd driven her home in. Something moved on her right. Roxie halted.

"It's only Luke," Johnny said, taking her arm.

His friend. Two against one, not good. And now he was pulling her along, double not good. Roxie dug her heels into the gravel lot. "Look. I'd rather stay over here in the light so I can see what I'm doing," she tried.

"Come on." Johnny gave her a tug to get her moving. "I have a light inside my car."

Roxie wanted to run. But she needed him to take the pills. And she needed to get the tape. In a flash of morbid thought Roxie took solace in knowing if something happened to her, Victoria would see that *Mami* was taken care of.

"Hey, Luke," Johnny said into the darkness. "Roxie said next time you don't have to hide."

"I said maybe there'd be a next time." *Maybe as in never, you miscreant.*

Johnny stopped beside an old-style Cadillac parked in the shadows and opened the door. She could sense Luke close by. Johnny rummaged through a bag on the backseat and took out what looked like a DVD in a clear plastic case.

"How do I know that's of me?" she asked.

He held it up to show her "Roxie" written in black marker on the disk. But wait a minute. "Shouldn't there be a tape? From the video recorder?"

Johnny smiled. "I told you she was smart, Luke," he said and turned back to the bag. He emerged with three mini-camcorder tapes.

She held out her hand.

He held the disk and tapes out of reach. "What do you have for me?"

Roxie felt around in her purse and pulled out two sheets of blister-packed Percocet pills and two of Vicodin pills. He reached for them.

"I give you the pills. You give me the tape. Like we agreed." Roxie's heart pounded. She could smell her own sweat. "At the same time."

Johnny stepped forward and held out the disk and tapes with his right hand. She took them with her left hand at the same time he snatched the pills from her right. There. It was done. But before relief could settle in, Johnny yanked her by the arm, turned her and forced her up against his car while he mashed his lips into hers.

"This is why you tried to screw me unconscious and insisted I take my pain medication afterward?" Fig's eerily calm voice penetrated the darkness. "If you want me to kiss you you're going to have to stop swapping spit with other men."

Oh, God. Not now. "It's not what you think," Roxie said, trying to push away from Johnny.

"Let her go," Fig demanded.

Johnny opened the front door of his car, reached inside and turned on his headlights, surrounding Fig in light. "Well, well, well. He sounds awful jealous for a patient," Johnny pointed out.

She should have inflicted a disorienting blow to his head when she'd had the chance.

"You told him I was your patient?" Fig asked. To anyone who didn't know him he'd come off completely calm and in control. But his right eye twitched, and his jaw looked made of stone.

"I don't want no trouble," Johnny said. "You can have her." He dropped his hands. "I'll just be on my way."

"No. Wait," Roxie said to him.

"You mean you want to come home with me and Luke, after all?"

"Roxie doesn't do tag team. Isn't that right,

honey?" Fig asked. "Or was that a lie, too? Maybe we're not as well matched in the bedroom as you led me to believe."

This was a nightmare. Wake up. Wake up.

"Get lost, buddy," Johnny said. "She's made her choice. Get in the car, Luke." Johnny grabbed Roxie around the waist and started to push her through the open door. "Come on, baby. Me and Luke. We got what you need."

"No." Roxie tried to twist free.

Fig started toward her.

Car after car skidded in around them.

Johnny pushed her away. "You double-crossing bitch." He slammed his gigantic fist into her cheek.

Pain exploded on contact. Tiny pinpricks of light speckled the darkness. A black nothingness threatened. Wanting to be finished with this whole situation, wanting to be done with this night, Roxie didn't fight it.

CHAPTER NINE

BACK at the hospital. Again. Fig paced the E.R. hallway outside of Roxie's room. He couldn't tell which hand hurt worse, the one attached to his fractured wrist or the one that'd planted the knock-out punch to the unchivalrous excuse for a man who'd struck Roxie.

"You are some piece of work." Kyle handed him a bag of ice. "You're going to need an X-ray, you know."

"Nothing's broken." Fig made a loose fist then, despite the pain, extended his fingers. "You haven't mentioned how you and Victoria happened to be in O'Halloran's parking lot at eleven-thirty on a Tuesday night. And why you didn't warn me what was going down."

"I don't know much more than you," Kyle said, his hands in his pockets. "I couldn't sleep on that couch Victoria banished me to, so I was awake when she tried to sneak out of the house."

"What is with the two of them?" Roxie, allowing herself to be used in some sting operation to capture a drug-dealing blackmailer—he found out after the fact—putting herself in danger. She and Victoria sneaking around, not confiding in the men responsible for protecting them.

Victoria stuck her head out into the hallway. "She's awake."

Finally. Some answers. Up to now all Victoria would say is "it's not my story to tell." Fig followed Kyle into Roxie's room, which looked identical to the one he'd been in prior to his surgery. She lay on a stretcher, the top slightly elevated, with no pillow. Her left eye was almost swollen shut, the area surrounding it and her cheek an inflamed red that made Fig want to search out the goon from the parking lot and hit him again. He was in the E.R. somewhere. Fig had seen him come in.

"You hit him?" Roxie accused the second she saw him.

"He hit you," Fig explained.

"With your left hand?"

He held up his splinted arm. "Well, I couldn't use my right."

"How are you going to take care of yourself?"

She was worried about him?

"And if you're both here—" she pointed back and forth between Kyle and Victoria "—who's home with *Mami* and Jake?"

"Ali and Jared," Victoria answered.

"Then who's watching the baby?" Roxie asked.

"They brought him along," Victoria said. "Your mother is in love."

Roxie flung her arm over her forehead. "You should all be in your own homes in your own beds."

"I had to be there," Victoria said, standing next to the stretcher. "In case something went wrong. If Ali wasn't nursing, she would have come, too. She and Jared had a huge argument over it."

"We'd have had a huge argument, too, *honey,*" Kyle said to Victoria, "if you'd taken the time to fill me in on your little plan."

"Which is why I didn't," Victoria countered.

"Would one of you please tell me what the heck is going on?" Fig asked. Loudly.

Roxie clamped her eyes closed and brought her hands up to her temples. "Keep it down, will ya? Lady with a closed head injury here."

"Sorry," he whispered.

"That's it. I'm going to start charging," she said to him. "Fifty dollars every time you do something that warrants an apology to me. Effective immediately." She held out her hand.

"Start me a tab," he said. "You know you're awful chipper for someone who was mauled and beaten in a dark parking lot."

"That little hit?" She waved him off. "My brothers used to hit me harder than that. He caught me by surprise is all."

One more reason to hate her brothers. "Can we focus on the reason you were in O'Halloran's parking lot to begin with? Why you snuck out of my bed to meet a blackmailer? Why half the town's police force and men in official-looking black cars knew about it and I didn't?" That last part hurt. Did she not think she could trust him? After everything they'd shared?

Roxie turned to face the wall. "I'd rather not talk about it."

"We'll wait outside," Victoria said, taking Kyle by the hand.

"But I want to know, too," Kyle complained.

Victoria pushed him out of the room.

After the door closed behind them, Roxie didn't move. "You didn't take your pain medicine."

He was a pro at faking it and pretending sleep. "You weren't yourself at dinner. You seemed antsy and distracted." The sex had been different, too. Dispassionate. Desperate. Almost impersonal.

"So you followed me?"

"If you'll remember, I asked you what was wrong." At least half a dozen times. "I was worried about you. Talk to me," Fig said quietly.

"I didn't want you to find out." She sounded so miserable his heart ached for her. "To know the truth."

"Whatever it is, it's okay." He approached the stretcher. "We'll get through it."

"We? We'll get through it?" She gave an emotionless chuckle. "You'd be wise to run or you'll get brought down right along with me. *Ay Dios mio.* Your parents will be in town to see it happen."

"I won't run. I can't. I'm falling in love with you, Roxie. And when you love someone…"

"You have known me barely two weeks. The worst damn two weeks of my miserable life, as it turns out. You're nuts to think you love me," she said. "Hell, I'm so screwed up right now *I* don't even love me."

"Roxie…"

"Don't 'Roxie' me, all calm as can be. I'm giving you an out. Take it. Trust me, you'll be glad you did."

"Let me help you."

She laughed. "You can't even help yourself. How are you going to help me? Come tomorrow everyone will know. I'll be even more of a pariah than I am now. And you, adding fuel to the fire. 'If you want me to kiss you you'll have to stop swapping spit with other men.'"

"I walked up to see you kissing another man. I'm sorry if the sight of it upset me."

"I was wearing a wire, Fig. Lord knows how many people heard you admit you couldn't bring yourself to kiss me because of where my mouth has been."

That's not what he'd said.

"I wonder how the newspaper will spin that in the not-so-flattering article they are sure to be working on as we speak. Hmmmm." She tapped her chin. "I can picture the headline. 'Not Only Is the Whack-Job Hoarder's House Too Filthy to

Live In, But She's Been with So Many Men Her Mouth is Too Dirty to Kiss.'"

"I'm sorry. I didn't mean…"

She turned away from him and held out her palm for another fifty dollars. "You can go now."

"Don't do this, Roxie. Don't push me away. Whatever has you so upset, it can't be as bad as you think."

"You have no idea."

"Maybe…"

"Maybe nothing. The police confiscated all the tapes from the video. In their entirety. And nothing stays secret in Madrin Falls."

"The video's old news. People have already seen it."

Roxie seemed to deflate. "Not all of it."

"What?"

She let out a deep breath. "There was more. Johnny only uploaded the first half."

Now it made sense. "He threatened to upload the second part."

She nodded. "This time I got in touch with Victoria, who worked with the hospital investigators, the DEA and the police to set up tonight's fun."

"But why? It's more of the same. No one's going to care."

"It is not more of the same," she snapped. "I let him do things to me. Perverted, embarrassing things. And I liked them," she said defiantly. "Before you, sex had become boring. Routine."

Before him. If she weren't so upset he would have puffed up with pride and smiled.

"I needed more," she continued. "Johnny offered me an opportunity to explore new avenues to find satisfaction and I accepted. Willingly. I enjoyed myself more than I had in months. Maybe years. Tomorrow everyone will know the full extent of just how freakishly screwed up I really am."

"Roxie. There's nothing wrong with experimenting." In fact the thought excited him. "With two consenting adults finding pleasure in a way that's agreeable to them both. You're not a freak. You're not screwed up."

"Says the man who refuses to kiss me because my mouth is too dirty, who won't let me cook for him because he thinks I'm out to poison him and who won't leave the house without hand sanitizer in his pocket. I'm sorry if your opinion of freakish behavior doesn't mean all that much."

Someone knocked at the door. Without waiting for a response Victoria stuck her head in. "The police are here, Roxie. They need to speak with you."

"Goodbye, Fig."

He did not like the finality in her tone. "I'll be right outside."

"No. I want you to leave. I'm tired. Exhausted, actually. I can barely handle my own problems without yours adding to the enormous mound. I've enjoyed playing temporary pretend girlfriend. But reality check. We're from two different worlds with enough baggage between us to sink an ocean liner. Focus on yourself. Fix yourself. Find a nice Jewish girl and have a nice perfect life."

Two police officers entered the room.

Victoria took him by the arm. "There'll be no changing her mind tonight." She guided him to the door. "When she's ready for discharge, I'll bring her home with me."

"But…"

"You need to come now," she whispered as they exited the room. "There's a reporter from the newspaper nosing around. Kyle's got him cornered in the lounge."

* * *

After driving for hours, not wanting to return to the condo to see reminders of Roxie and feel the loss and frustration of not being able to hold her, comfort her and reassure her, Fig pulled into the parking lot of the only decent motel in town. He sat for a few minutes, wondering if this was the right thing to do, and decided, yes. It was time. Past time. He wanted to be the man Roxie confided in, trusted with all her secrets and turned to with confidence when she needed help. He wanted to enrich her life, not add to her burdens. To do that he had to start somewhere. So he got out of his car, climbed the stairs to the second floor, walked halfway down the row of rooms and knocked on his parents' door.

Roxie awoke to a large hand gently shaking her shoulder. "Time to wake up," a male voice said, startling her.

"Hey," the voice said. "It's okay. It's me. Kyle."

Kyle? In her bedroom? She lifted her head, and pain sliced through it. "Ow." She tried to open her eyes. The left one achieved only a squint. Memories of last night came pouring back. Johnny. The punch. The complete video in the hands of the police. Victoria's old, like-sleeping-on-burlap-covered-straw couch.

And Fig. Gone. Because she'd pushed him away. Because he'd let her.

The pain traveled to her heart.

"I was told to wake you up by nine," Kyle said, standing over her.

"Nine?" Roxie sat up. "Where's *Mami?*"

"Shoot," Kyle said. "Would you lie back down?"

Roxie looked up at him to see if he was serious.

He held up notepaper with Victoria's neat handwriting on it. "Number two," Kyle said. "I was supposed to help you sit up in case you got dizzy."

Roxie smiled. That was Victoria, Miss Organization/Delegation. "I'm not dizzy," Roxie said. "What's number three?"

"Bring you fresh water." He pointed to a glass on the coffee table. "Four. Offer you acetaminophen or ibuprofen in case your head hurts." He pointed to two pill bottles beside the water. "Five. Make you breakfast. Six. Tell you to read the newspaper. Seven. Get you to your house by ten."

"Well, check, check, check and check." She picked up the newspaper from the coffee table and flung it, Frisbee style, into the open stairwell leading to the front door. "You can cross me reading that rag off your list. Not gonna happen."

"You hungry?" Kyle asked.

"No."

"Okay. I'll make you some toast." He pointed to his list. "You see this small writing here? Victoria said not to take no for an answer." He turned toward the kitchen.

"Can you say whipped?" Roxie called after him.

"Whipped. And enjoying every minute of it. Well, except for sleeping on the couch. There are fresh towels in the bathroom if you want to shower."

"Why's it so quiet here?" Roxie asked. "Where is everyone?"

"Victoria has your mom and Jake over at your house."

"What?" Roxie jumped up. The room spun. "Whoa." She plopped back down.

Kyle stuck his head out of the kitchen. "If you fall down and hurt yourself I'm going to be royally pissed."

"*Mami*'s not strong enough. Her heart. What was Victoria thinking?" She popped the cap on the acetaminophen and swallowed back a few with a water chaser.

"Relax. Have you ever known Victoria to over-look a detail? Jared changed shifts with another doc. He'll be on-site for the duration of your mom's visit. And he pilfered some stuff from the E.R. just in case."

Roxie fingered the swollen tissue on her face. "What did you tell *Mami* about my eye?"

"That you got hit trying to stop a father from beating his son outside the convenience mart."

Genius. Roxie smiled. "Who thought of that?"

"You're welcome," Kyle said with a smile of his own.

"Now all we have to do is keep her away from the newspaper."

"Victoria hid her glasses."

Ten minutes later Roxie had freshened up and was ready to go. "I need a ride," she said on her way out the door.

"You're going to get me into trouble for not feed-ing you." Kyle followed after her, holding a piece of toast.

Roxie stopped short, surprised to see her red car parked in Victoria's driveway.

"Fig drove it over from the bar," Kyle said. "And he borrowed my pickup, so I'll drive you in your car."

Roxie fished her keys out of her oversize bag. "I'm perfectly capable of…"

Kyle plucked them from her hand. "Number eight. I'm to drive because your vision is impaired."

"Does that woman miss anything?"

"Actually, Fig added that one."

She turned to Kyle. "Fig?" He didn't hate her? Hadn't left town?

"The calls started coming in around five this morning."

Welcome to small-town U.S.A. "Threats to run me out of town? Reports of cross burnings on my lawn?"

"If you want to know, read the article in the paper."

Not a chance.

"He was here by six-thirty and he and Victoria set to work making lists. Newsflash, Fig can be almost as anal as Victoria is."

"God help us," Roxie joked.

"Have a care with his heart," Kyle said seriously.

"I've never seen him as upset as he was last night when you went down. And we've been through a lot together."

"You would honestly let your friend get involved with someone like me?" Roxie asked. The town's good-time girl?

"Fig is a very good judge of character," Kyle answered. "And for the record, I was the one who encouraged him to come for a visit to meet you. Now get in the car. We're on a tight schedule."

Kyle turned onto her street and Roxie couldn't believe the congestion, cars and trucks lining the sidewalks. A news van sat parked on her neighbor's lawn. "This is a nightmare," she said, envisioning pandemonium when she stepped out of the car. Cameras flashing. People yelling taunts and insults. "Nothing better to do on a Wednesday morning? Worthless busybodies. Doesn't anyone work a day job anymore?"

Kyle squeezed the car into a space between her neighbor's chain-link fence and the portable carport Roxie had erected to hide the grotesque pile of discarded children's toys and equipment *Mami* had accumulated.

"Come to think of it," Roxie continued. "Why aren't you at work? And Victoria? Is that Ali on the front lawn? She's on maternity leave. She shouldn't be here. And if Jared's here and that's Ali's gramps standing next to her, who's watching little James? Have you all gone insane?"

"We're your friends, Roxie. We're all here today because you need us to be." Kyle reached down between his seat and the door and handed her the newspaper he'd tried to foist on her earlier. "Now stop being a pain in the ass and read the damn article. You made the front page." He unfolded it and held it open in front of her face. "Number six on my list. Read it."

"'Local Nurse a Local Hero Who Needs Our Help.'" Roxie read the headline. A blown up, black-and-white copy of her hospital ID badge photo was centered beneath it. "What?" She looked at Kyle.

He smiled.

Roxie looked through the car window to see that while some people were standing around watching the spectacle, the majority were working. *Mami* sat in a chair on the porch with Jake at her side. A blonde woman Roxie recognized from the hospital came out of the house carrying a large white garbage bag. She stopped in front of *Mami,* who examined the bag, which Roxie knew would be labeled with the name of the person it was intended for. *Mami* nodded and pointed. The blonde walked to Victoria, who stood in the middle of the fray with a clipboard. Victoria pointed to the left. The woman walked to a sign with Ernesto's name on it and set the bag on the pile.

"Victoria's carrying a clipboard," Roxie noted.

"She loves to be in charge, that woman of mine." Kyle looked out the window at his fiancée. "Look over there."

Roxie looked in the direction of his finger. "Jeez Louise. Fig has one, too."

"Read the rest. I'm stuck hostage until you do because I can't open my door. So get to it." He looked at his watch. "Number seven. Get you to the house by ten. I have eight minutes."

Roxie scanned the article. "Local nurse the victim of a sexual predator/narcotics dealer…volunteered to help catch him without regard for her reputation or personal safety… As a result, law enforcement obtained records and videotapes implicating the suspect and an accomplice in fraudulent activities at dozens of hospitals across New York State… The hero and her mother need our help."

"I was a victim?"

"Yes. You were." Kyle crossed something off his list. "And if Fig chose to play around with the facts a bit, so be it. He can be a master manipulator when it suits him."

"It's in his genes."

"But he uses it for the greater good. Speak of the devil."

Roxie's door opened and there stood Fig, dressed in work clothes and a baseball cap. He held out his left palm to help her out of the car. Roxie flipped it over and kissed his still-slightly-swollen, bruised knuckles before exiting.

Kyle climbed out behind her.

Fig kissed her left cheek gently. "Does it hurt?" he asked quietly and kissed her temple.

Not anymore. He kissed her forehead. Her nose. He set his right cheek to hers, the corners of their mouths almost touching. "Don't give up on me, Roxie," he whispered. "I'm going to beat it. I'm going to be a man you're proud to be with."

He already was.

"I love you," he said. "It came out of nowhere.

I didn't plan for it to happen. But here we are. I spent a miserable night without you, not knowing what today would bring."

From the minute he'd exited her hospital room, Roxie had been miserable, too. But, "You can't. It's too soon."

"Yes, I can." He shifted to look at her face. "We've been through so much in such a short time. I know what I feel. It's okay if you don't…"

"If worrying about you and wanting to take care of you and missing you every minute we're not together means I love you, then I do. But…"

"No buts." Fig touched a finger to her lips. "For now let's just leave it at we love each other. We'll work the rest out later."

A horn honking "La Cucaracha" had everyone stopping what they were doing to look out at the street in front of the house. A refurbished 1960s-style car with gleaming chrome fenders pulled to a stop, and a huge Latino man climbed out of the front passenger door.

"Which one's that?" Fig asked.

"What do you mean which one? I don't recognize him. It's not like I know every man in town." She tried to step away.

"Stop," Fig said. "You have to stop twisting what I say. Which brother is that?"

"That's one of my brothers?" *Ay Dios mio*. He did not look happy. "This was a bad idea."

Fig waved him over.

"Stop that. What the heck are you doing?"

"We need to finish this, Roxie. Today's the day."

Two equally huge men climbed out of the back-seat and the driver drove off. Roxie glanced at the condition of the house and yard, mortified it looked nothing like it had fifteen years earlier.

Fig stepped forward to greet her brothers.

Roxie headed for the porch, grabbing Jared on the way. "You got a defibrillator somewhere? My brothers showed up, after all." Even if *Mami* didn't need it, Roxie might.

"It's going to be fine." Jared wrapped an arm around her shoulders. "Ali." His wife looked up from stacking hundreds of plastic take-out containers. "You got my bags?" Ali nodded.

Roxie climbed the steps. *"Hola, Mami,"* she said.

Her mother stood and took Roxie's face between her hands. *"Mi querida hija.* Look at your beautiful face. That man should be arrested."

"Sit. I need to tell you something."

"Mami," a loud booming voice called out.

Roxie recognized that voice, Roberto, her oldest, meanest brother, and froze, scared to look at him.

Her mother clutched her chest and grabbed for the broken porch railing. Jared reached out to steady her. "Keep breathing, Mrs. Morano." Ali walked up beside Roxie and rubbed her back. "You, too, Rox."

"Funny how you could be a grown, independent woman one second and feel like a scared five-year-old girl the next," she whispered to Ali as her brother's large stride ate up the distance to the porch.

"It's going to be okay," Ali said.

Roxie knew better.

"Hey, bug eyes," Roberto said when he reached her. "Great job taking care of the home front."

Bug eyes. No one dared call her that to her face in years. How he used to make her cry.

"Roberto, mi hijo," Mami said with reverence, reaching up a hand to touch him as if to confirm he was real and not an apparition.

"Si, Mami. And I brought Miguel, Cruz and Ernesto with me. We'll have this place cleaned out and fixed up in no time."

"You can't…" *Just come in here and take over,* Roxie wanted to say.

But *Mami* said, "See, Roxie. I told you they'd come."

Roberto flashed an evil smile from over *Mami's* shoulder as he bent to hug her.

Why exactly did they come? Roxie wondered. Why now, when she'd called each one of them so many times over the years without so much as a call back from all but Ernesto? What had Fig done?

"Will you two keep an eye on *Mami?*" Roxie asked Jared and Ali, who both nodded. Confident her mother was in good hands, she went to find Fig, taking the long way around the yard to avoid her other brothers—having no desire to see Ernesto in particular after the nasty messages he'd left on her cell phone after "accidentally coming across" her video online.

She slipped in between two small box trucks… and ran into Fig's parents on the sidewalk.

A bullet between the eyes seemed like the only way to improve upon this day. She forced a smile. "Hello, Mr. and Mrs. Figelstein. What brings you here?" *Come to see Roxie's beautiful home? To meet her warm, welcoming family? To see what a wonderful choice your son has made in picking a woman to fall in love with?*

To Roxie's complete and utter shock, Fig's mother flung herself at Roxie's chest and clamped her arms around her midback, pinning Roxie's arms at her sides. Roxie briefly contemplated the best defensive wrestling maneuvers to ward off the unprovoked attack and escape the pythonlike squeeze without hurting the smaller woman, until Mrs. Figelstein said, "Thank you. For convincing Ryan to come talk to me. For giving me back my son."

That's when Roxie realized Fig's mother was actually hugging her…and how good it felt to be hugged right then. And she burst into tears. Not the ladylike kind, either. "I'm sorry." She'd been holding in so much for so long it was getting harder and harder to contain all the emotion. She tried to pull away so she could go someplace private to get herself together. "It's been a difficult few days."

Fig's mom didn't let go. "There, there." She patted between Roxie's shoulder blades like she was burping a baby. "Ryan's told us what you've been going through. You get it all out, honey. Albert. My purse. Get the dear girl some tissues."

Honey? Dear girl? Self-pity outburst over. Somewhere between the front of the box trucks and the rear, she'd slipped into an alternate reality.

"What's going on here?" Fig yelled. "What did you do?" He peeled his mother off and pulled Roxie into his arms.

"She didn't do anything." Roxie sniffled. "I kind of lost it for a minute."

"Jared told me what happened." He ran his fingers through her hair and eased her head to his shoulder. "I'm sorry."

She held out her hand for a fifty.

"Will you take it in trade?" he asked quietly.

She nodded. And felt her spirits lift instantly.

"Look at that, Albert. Our Ryan is in love."

Fig let out a breath. "A few more days and they'll all be gone," he whispered.

"What if we don't survive it?" Roxie whispered back.

"I hear you make a chicken soup with matzo balls that will make me weep," Mrs. Figelstein said. "That's a very important skill for a woman running a Jewish household. Have you considered converting?"

Roxie lifted her head and looked at Fig. "Did she just…?"

Fig raised his eyebrows and nodded. "Yup."

"We don't have to make any decisions now," his mother added.

"We?" Roxie asked Fig quietly.

"As long as she's willing to raise the children Jewish. You are, aren't you, Roxie?"

"Am I pregnant and don't know it?" Roxie whispered.

"Enough, Mom," Fig warned. "Did you do what I asked?"

"Sandwiches, drinks and chips for one hundred will be delivered promptly at noon."

"I said for fifty," Fig clarified.

"Well, dear. I made Daddy drive me past on our way to the deli and it's a good thing I did. No self-respecting Jewish mother would ever host a party that did not provide enough food for everyone in attendance. You remember that, Roxie. Now come." She took Roxie by the arm. "Introduce me to your mother."

That was a terrible idea. "I don't think…"

Someone yelled out, "Roxie." Ali.

And Roxie ran.

Mami, who'd been doing so well since the fire, sat in her chair, rocking and looking down at the ground. "What happened?" Roxie asked, dropping to her knees at *Mami's* feet.

"I wanted to show them," *Mami* mumbled. "I decide. It's not all garbage."

"Si, Mami," Roxie agreed. "They're your things. You decide. Just like on the TV show."

"But look." *Mami* pointed to her brothers, who stood amidst the now organized mess of her front yard, pitching bag after bag haphazardly into the back of a box truck like they were tossing trash into a Dumpster.

"Stop," Roxie yelled, walking to her brothers. "These are *Mami's* things that she's collected for you for years." She lowered her voice. "While I couldn't care less what you do with them after you drive them away, you will respect them, and respect her wishes while you're here."

"You going to make us, Roxie?" Ernesto asked, his words oozing contempt. "Or are you going by a porn name these days?"

"Sticks and stones," Mrs. Figelstein said from beside her, then Fig's mother opened fire. "You ought to be ashamed of yourself." She took on

Ernesto. "Talking to your little sister like that. The poor girl was drugged and abused and it was an absolutely horrific experience for her."

The woman had Jewish guilt down.

Ernesto looked stricken.

"The four of you, coming here and upsetting your mother. Get down from that truck," she demanded. When Roberto didn't move she yelled, "Right. Now," in a voice worthy of a military drill sergeant. And well, what do you know? Her big, tough bully of a brother listened. "You all go and apologize." She pointed to the porch. "This. Instant."

Roxie leaned in to Fig. "Your family is awful big on apologies."

He gave her a small half smile.

"Move it," Fig's mother said with authority, as if anyone who didn't would suffer severe consequences.

Her brothers didn't know what to make of her—a vicious ankle biter yapping at four Rottweilers, holding them entranced. Then they looked at Fig's dad, who may not talk much but stood tall and protective behind his wife. They glanced from Jared and Ali, who stood on the porch with *Mami,* to

Roxie and Fig, Victoria and Kyle and dozens of other friends and coworkers and even some towns-people she'd never met, who'd all come to stand beside her.

For the first time in her life, Roxie didn't have to go it alone. She felt weak with relief.

Fig stepped forward to confront her brothers in semiprivate. "The terms you all agreed to were you come home, make nice and clean out the house without upsetting your mother. You want me to stick to my end of our deal you'd better stick to yours."

"You're right, ma'am," one of her brothers, either Miguel or Cruz, said to Fig's mom. And he led the other three up to the porch to *Mami*.

"She's amazing," Roxie said to Fig.

He actually looked a little proud as he watched his mom follow Roxie's brothers. "She has her mo-ments."

"So you had a nice talk with her?"

"Most of the night. I'm sorry she brought up…"

Roxie held out her hand. "I think that makes two hundred dollars you owe me. How *will* you work it off?" she teased.

"The only way to find out is if you come home

with me at the end of the day." He looked hopeful. But was prolonging their relationship really the way to go? So they loved each other. He didn't live in Madrin Falls, and Roxie couldn't leave *Mami* and couldn't afford, nor did she want to hire on, a live-in caregiver. It was her responsibility to care for her mother.

"I know how to make you say yes," Fig said. He leaned close. "Sorry. Sorry. Sorry. Sorry. Sorry. There," he said. "That will keep me busy all night long."

He was right, that did get her to say yes. And after a brief nap when they got back to his place, he did keep busy. All. Night. Long.

CHAPTER TEN

ON THURSDAY morning, after answering a knock on the condo door, Fig said goodbye to the mysterious visitor he did not invite in and turned to her, holding out a police evidence bag containing a DVD with her name on it and three small camcorder cassettes. The same ones Johnny had given her and the police had later retrieved from her purse and taken into evidence while she'd been unconscious.

Was it possible? Could the nightmare of Johnny be over without Madrin Falls—and the internet porn-loving community at large—being privy to a second installment?

As if he could read her mind, Fig smiled and nodded.

Roxie ran to him and threw her arms around his neck. "How did you…?"

He hugged her close. "All I'm at liberty to share is I acquired them through legal means, they are no longer evidence and can be dealt with as you see fit."

Bonfire! "Thank you." She kissed his neck. "I can't tell you how much this means to me."

"Then why don't you show me?" Fig suggested, stepping back.

They'd been at it most of the night. Even she was exhausted, and she hadn't undergone major surgery a few days prior. "You can't possibly…"

Instead of walking to the bedroom like she'd first thought, Fig stopped at the hall closet, took out a second bag, this one a nondescript red plastic shopping bag with handles, and walked it over to her.

Roxie peeked inside. Couldn't believe it. She looked up at Fig.

"I don't know what went on after the first few minutes of the video," he said, taking her back into his arms—her new favorite place to be. "And I don't care. But if you want to play and experiment I'm all in. If this bag doesn't contain what you're looking for, then we'll keep shopping until we find it."

How was she ever going to leave him when it came time to return home with *Mami?* For the next ten days they lived like honeymooners, working at her house during the day and indulging each other's sexual fantasies at night.

On day one, Fig started counseling four times a week.

On day two, *Mami* agreed to attend counseling.

On day three, *Mami* canceled the counseling appointment Roxie had made on day two.

On day four, her brothers returned to their homes, *Papi*'s and their secondhand "booty" transported out of town in the three small box trucks that'd been parked in front of her house, one driven away by Roberto, one by Ernesto and one by Cruz.

No tearful goodbyes there. But Ernesto did apologize for his porn comment and promised to stay in touch.

On day five, Fig's parents returned home, after garnering Roxie and Fig's assurances that they'd visit within the next two weeks. With *Mami*.

On days six, seven, eight and nine, Roxie's house was repaired and outfitted with new flooring and carpeting, a fresh coat of paint and a brand-new kitchen. All covered by insurance.

But like every brief bit of good in Roxie's life, on day ten reality intervened to put an end to her happiness.

"I don't want to go," she said to Fig over a delicious farewell breakfast of mushroom-and-Swiss-cheese omelets.

"It's not the end of us," Fig emphasized.

But it was the end of spending their nights, mornings and evenings together. Just the two of them. It was the end of impromptu private discussions and cuddle sessions on the couch. Roxie picked at the half of her omelet her stomach refused to accept.

"We'll see each other every day." Fig reached out to take her cold hand into his warm one.

But it wouldn't be the same.

"We'll find a way to make it work, Roxie." He squeezed.

"But your job and your apartment. I can't ask you to stick around Madrin Falls knowing it may be years before I can give you more than a few stolen hours here and there." She felt her face heat. "I mean, assuming that's what you want."

Fig released her hand, slid back his chair and patted his lap. "Come."

She loved that even at almost six feet tall she wasn't too big to curl up on Fig's lap.

He wrapped his arms around her and kissed her head through her hair. "You didn't ask me to stay,

I offered. Yes, I'd like more than a few stolen hours here and there, but I understand your situation. I applaud your dedication to caring for your mother. And I'm willing to take whatever time you have available to keep you in my life. I love you." He kissed her head again.

"I love you, too," Roxie said. So much. Partly because he accepted her decision to move back in with *Mami* without trying to change her mind. Because if he'd asked her not to, if he'd suggested she hire a caretaker and invited her to live with him full-time, she may not have been able to refuse.

That night they exchanged "I love yous" again— via cell phone—each alone in their own bed. As Roxie had suspected, it wasn't the same. Her heart—heck, her entire body and soul—ached for him.

Two days later, after rising early to clean up *Mami*'s breakfast mess in the kitchen then working her first twelve-hour shift in weeks, Roxie returned home to find four garbage bags of clothes, an old plastic dollhouse and a slightly rusted scooter on the brand-new beige carpeting of her living room.

"What is this?" she yelled at the top of her lungs.

Mami walked in from the direction of her bedroom, where she'd spent most of her time since they'd returned home, despite the family room being completely accessible and fully functional with new slipcovers on the sofas and a brand-new TV—a housewarming gift from Fig.

"They're from the church," *Mami* answered as if Roxie hadn't seen hundreds of similar bags before. Served her right for asking a stupid question.

"No." Roxie put her hands on her hips. "They are not staying. We talked about this. It took dozens of people four days to clean out this house. We both agreed we never wanted to go through that again."

"It's only a few things. For the next time the boys come."

Not again. Please, not again. Roxie's insides felt hollow except for a blistering hot ball of despair deep in her gut.

Mami scanned the room. "We have plenty of space now. If it upsets you I can put them in the boys' room." She started to drag one of the bags down to the raccoon room, as she and Fig now referred to it.

"Stop," Roxie said.

She did.

Right then and there Roxie made a decision. "I won't stay here if you continue to take in donations from the church. Either I load this stuff into my car this minute and I'll drop it back at the church tomorrow on my way home from work, or I'm moving out."

"You won't even know it's here." *Mami* dragged the first bag down the hall.

Yes, she would. "You need help to deal with this problem, *Mami*." Roxie's eyes filled with tears. "I will drive you to counseling. I will shop for you and take you to the doctor and church. I will continue to pay the bills. I will hire on a person to stay here with you so you're not alone. But I refuse to live here day after day and watch this house go to ruin. Not again."

Mami returned to the family room and dragged a second bag and then a third down the hall without further comment.

Roxie went into her bedroom to pack.

Fig glanced at his watch. Again.

"What's up with you?" Kyle asked from across the kitchen table.

"Today was Roxie's first day back at work. She was supposed to call when she got home." Two hours ago.

"Did her dirtbag brothers cash their checks?"

"Yeah."

Kyle shook his head. "Man, I don't believe it. Forty thousand dollars gone like that." He snapped.

Not that Fig minded spending it, and its loss in no way impacted his life, but he'd honestly—and mistakenly, as it turned out—thought to entice her brothers with the money, but once they arrived and witnessed the devastation firsthand, they'd do the right thing out of a sense of family, not monetary gain.

Wrong.

"How'd she react to you having to pay her brothers to come home?" Kyle asked, taking another cookie and dunking it in his coffee.

"She doesn't know."

"I think she suspects," Kyle said.

Because she's so smart and observant. "Maybe. But I fed her a story that I called each brother and told them I was the producer of a nationally syndicated hoarding show, and I was scheduled to begin filming on location at Roxie's house. That I did a pretend interview with questions intended to enrage them and provoke them to return home to clean out the house before taping for the show began."

In fact he'd tried that scenario with Roberto. Who'd called him some—what he suspected were—choice names in Spanish, then told him to go to hell so there'd be no misunderstanding. But Fig refused to let Roxie down. So he'd spoken in the universal language of U.S. currency.

Someone knocked on the door. Fig opened it to find Roxie, her eyes wet and rimmed in red, holding two overstuffed duffel bags, looking seconds from breaking down.

At the sight of him she dropped her bags and lunged toward him.

Fig opened his arm to catch her.

She held him tight. "Do you think it'd be okay for me to stay with you for a few days?"

Forever. "For as long as you want."

She said, "Thank you," then started to cry.

He eased her into the condo so Kyle could scoot out the door to drag in the duffels then leave.

"I can't do it," she said in between hiccuping breaths. "Not again." Fig calmed her down enough to explain what had her so upset.

"Who's with your mom now?" he asked.

"I arranged for her friend from church to stay

with her for a few days. But I'll need to make more permanent arrangements."

"Tomorrow," Fig said. "We'll take care of it tomorrow."

He walked her to the couch and pulled her down onto his lap.

"I like it when you say 'we.'" She cuddled into his chest.

"Well, I like saying 'we,'" Fig said. And he liked being part of a "we."

Roxie looked up at him, her eyes sad. "Thank you," she said. "For taking me in. For understanding me and knowing me—the real me—and still loving me."

"And thank *you*," Fig said in return. "For taking *me* into your heart. For understanding me and accepting me—the real me—and still loving me right back."

Then, staring deeply into the loving brown eyes of the woman he planned to spend the rest of his life with, Fig knew no time would be more perfect. So without a care for germs or bacteria or sickness, with his full focus on showing the woman in his arms how much he truly loved her and wanted her in his life, Fig dipped his head and set his lips to hers.

EPILOGUE

Three months later

"Sí. Sí. Adiós, Mami," Roxie said, ending the call.

Fig put down his book and watched her pad barefoot across the white tile floor of their two-week beachfront vacation rental to drop her phone in her purse on the kitchen counter. Then she joined him out on the lanai, bending beneath the huge umbrella to remove his baseball cap and kiss the top of his head. "Fight it all you want, my love. But in the three days we've been here, you have actually started to get some color."

Yeah. An unappealing, unattractive, uncool pink.

She walked to the edge of their small wooden patio and stared out to the ocean less than one hundred feet away. "This is so much more beautiful than I'd ever imagined."

"It's exactly as I'd imagined it." Heat. Sand. Salty air. The beautiful blue-green water and palm trees he'd seen only in pictures. A completely relaxed

Roxie wearing a teeny, tiny, hot-pink string bikini, showing lots of deliciously smooth, deeply tanned skin, adorned with a dangling gold belly button ring, sipping an iced strawberry margarita. Beautiful curves, enchanting smiles and contagious laughter. Perfection.

"How's your mom doing?" Fig asked.

Roxie slid the wicker chair beside him into full sun and sat down. "The change is unbelievable. Marvela—" who now lived with Roxie's mother and, in lieu of rent, supervised and assisted her "—has them both volunteering at a local day care twice a week. *Mami* is the on-site grandma for the three-year-olds." Roxie sipped her icy beverage. "At an invite from Ali's gramps, she's attending activities at the senior center, and she's knitting afghans and baby blankets for the women's crisis center. I've never heard her so happy." Roxie set her drink in a shady spot and reclined, tilting her face up to the sun. "It's like my moving out improved her quality of life."

"Finally agreeing to attend therapy improved her quality of life," Fig said. "You taking a stand shocked her into compliance."

"If only I'd done it sooner. All those years…"

"Nuh, uh, uh," Fig said. "The past is in the past. Nothing we can do about it today."

She held up a hand to shade her eyes and looked at him. "Stop throwing my words back at me."

He smiled. "They're good words." That Fig had needed to hear a few times himself—well, in addition to a couple of dozen counseling sessions—before he'd effectively tucked his past into a pocket of his memory, never to be lamented over or angered by again.

"Victoria's pregnant," Roxie said. "Jake blurted it out when they had *Mami* over to dinner on Friday."

Fig was happy for his friends. "That's what she and Kyle wanted." He eyed Roxie. "What about you? Do you want children?"

She laughed. "Could you imagine me a mother?"

Actually, yes, he could. "I think you'd make a terrific mother." Loving. Attentive. Dependable.

"I think I'd be annoyingly strict," she said with a scowl.

"Good," Fig said. "I'll be the fun parent." She balled up her napkin and threw it at him.

"I have a surprise for you." He handed Roxie the rectangular box with the now flattened red bow he'd stashed in his shorts pocket that morning. "I thought maybe we could try out something new tonight."

Roxie smiled—bless her adventurous soul—sat up and plucked the box from his hand. She shook it and held it up to her ear. "Fur-lined nipple clamps?"

Next time. "You'll have to open it to find out."

She pulled one end of the ribbon to unravel the bow then undid the knot and dropped it on the table. She lifted the lid. At the sight of all the pink tissue paper stuffed inside she looked up at him like he was playing some type of prank. "Is there even anything in here?"

"Keep looking."

She took out each small piece of crumpled paper until she came upon the one that contained her surprise and began to unwrap it.

Fig went down on one knee at her feet.

"Ay Dios mio," she said in awe, at the two-carat teardrop diamond engagement ring he'd bought for her.

Fig took it from her hand. "Roxie Morano, knowing you has changed my life." He held the ring out to her. "I look forward to each new day, knowing you'll be a part of it. I love you more than anything. And if you'll do me the honor of becoming my wife, I will devote the rest of my life to taking care of you and making you happy."

Rather than the thrilled expression he'd hoped for, Roxie looked confused. "I thought you said this was for tonight?"

"It is." He kissed her knuckles. "I was hoping we could try out making love as an engaged couple. That's something we haven't done before. What do you think?"

"Are you sure?" she asked, hesitantly extending her fingers.

Fig looked up at her. "I'm sure." He slid the ring into place. "I love you, Roxie. Will you marry me?"

"Lord help you, Fig. I hope you don't live to regret this." She jumped up and pulled him up with her. "Yes." She flung her arms around his neck. "Yes, I'll marry you. And I promise to take care of you and try my hardest to make you happy right back."

Thank you. Fig let out a relieved breath and hugged her close. "I made reservations at the nicest restaurant in town so we could celebrate island style."

Roxie pulled back a bit to look at him. "I kind

of miss our cozy dinners when you used to cook for me every night." She caressed his head. "Do you think we could eat in tonight?"

She rubbed against him.

"Anything you want."

"I'd like that chocolate pudding pie you make for dessert."

He smiled, grabbing her butt with one hand and holding her still so he could do a little rubbing of his own. "The one with the whipped cream?" That she liked to "eat" in bed?

"Yeah," she said a little breathlessly as she rocked into his touch. "That's the one. Ya know—" she set her fingertips to his shoulders "—you're starting to feel a little hot. I think you need some more suntan lotion."

Their favorite tropical form of foreplay. Fig feared he'd go hard at the scent of coconut from now on. "But that always leads to..." he said innocently as he guided her to the sturdier of the two chaise longues, pulling at the strings of her top on the way.

"Exactly," Roxie said as she untied the strings of her bikini bottom, exposing the fist-size raccoon tattoo on her right butt check.

Fig pushed down his shorts and stepped out of them, thankful for the good sense that prompted him to pay extra for the most secluded cabin available.

And under the late-afternoon sun, to the sound of the ocean waves crashing into the shore, covered head to toe in protective SPF 50, Fig made love to his fiancée, in a way he was sure she'd never been made love to before.

* * * * *